# A HORSE AT THE WINDOW

# A HORSE
# AT THE
# WINDOW

## SPENCER GORDON

ANANSI

Published in Canada in 2024 and the USA in 2024 by House of Anansi Press Inc.
houseofanansi.com

House of Anansi Press is committed to protecting our natural environment.
This book is made of material from well-managed FSC®-certified forests,
recycled materials, and other controlled sources.

House of Anansi Press is a Global Certified Accessible™ (GCA by Benetech) publisher.
The ebook version of this book meets stringent accessibility standards
and is available to readers with print disabilities.

28 27 26 25 24    1 2 3 4 5

Library and Archives Canada Cataloguing in Publication

Title: A horse at the window / Spencer Gordon.
Names: Gordon, Spencer, 1984- author.
Description: Short stories.
Identifiers: Canadiana (print) 20240309553 | Canadiana (ebook) 20240309561
ISBN 9781487012502 (softcover) | ISBN 9781487012519 (EPUB)
Subjects: LCGFT: Short stories.
Classification: LCC PS8613.O735 H67 2024 | DDC C813/.6—dc23

Book design: Greg Tabor
Cover image: Mario Sánchez Nevado, https://marionevado.art

*House of Anansi Press is grateful for the privilege to work on and create from the Traditional Territory of many Nations,
including the Anishinabeg, the Wendat, and the Haudenosaunee, as well as the Treaty Lands of the
Mississaugas of the Credit.*

 **Canada Council Conseil des Arts
for the Arts du Canada**  ONTARIO ARTS COUNCIL
CONSEIL DES ARTS DE L'ONTARIO
an Ontario government agency
un organisme du gouvernement de l'Ontario

With the participation of the Government of Canada
Avec la participation du gouvernement du Canada |

*We acknowledge for their financial support of our publishing program the Canada Council for the Arts,
the Ontario Arts Council, and the Government of Canada.*

Printed and bound in Canada

FSC
www.fsc.org

MIX
Paper from
responsible sources
FSC® C103567

*Bhikkhus, all is burning. And what is the all that is burning?*
　　　　—Shakyamuni Buddha, the Ādittapariyāya Sutta (SN 35.28), translated from the Pali by Ñānamoli Thera

*I can connect*
*Nothing with nothing.*
　　　　—T. S. Eliot, "The Fire Sermon," *The Waste Land*

*I am in no way rebellious. I am in no way contrarian.*
*I just want people to like me.*
　　　　—Kristen Stewart

*If one has no determination, then it will be like catching*
*a glimpse of a horse galloping past the window:*
*in the twinkling of an eye it will be gone.*
　　　　—Mumon Ekai, "Mumon's Preface," *Mumonkan*, translated by Katsuki Sekida

Content note: The piece "Late Capitalism" contains scenes of torture and sexual violence.

# CONTENTS

1. Aperture I       1

"Ame ni mo Makezu"       4

Hypoarousal       7

Sandōkai, Non-Binary       12

Me First       16

Late Capitalism       19


2. Aperture II       25

Reasons for My Success       28

Hands and Eyes       32

The Chaos Magician       34

Cadets-in-Training Presentation, Toronto Police College, 2020       37

Motivation       45


3. The Garbage and Oil Thread       51


4. The Hell of Laughter       67

Joy Is Always with You       74

The Horrible Inclemency of Life       76

Memorial Prayer                                  81
This Thing I Believe                             85
Okay                                             89


5. The Gateless Gate                             93
Yes and No                                       96
Turn Your Anger into Sadness                     99
In the 2000s                                     101
There Is Nothing to Dislike                      113
The Fire Sermon                                  115


*Notes*                                          126
*Acknowledgements*                               132

I

# APERTURE I

THE WIND RATTLES the fence. The ground scrounges water. Overhead, in the grey, cloud-weary air, geese vee in sloppy formation, decrying the drabness of the world below. Their statements come flat and nasal and agree with your general disposition, which is to squint like a diminished peasant in a field sodden and fallow. Starvation is inevitable but not unkind. Cold, you move among the crushed garbage of spring. Crows grow preposterously fat atop the banging dumpsters. A dump truck idles in the pharmacy lot, and a swollen man in a reflective vest sucks nicotine, his pinched fingers scoured red. All around you are signs and letters, as plain and invisible as a lost pair of glasses sitting on your face. "I have lost my head," you call out, honking like the migrating geese, and are ignored, as voices fold into plastic.

We're where the sun settles over the fenceline and the dandelions begin and end, rippling over one another in dogged convulsions of birth and dying. A rabbit, smaller than a kitten, noses a petal, and blackbirds scatter notes on an empty clef. Sharp, minor, jagged treble, existing nowhere but in your head. It seems the earth is sighing, blowing your sunburns with tulip perfumes, and everything thrives without your touch. The wide world can go on without you, but *this* one—this one dome of green and blue, this single smear of bulbing pollen, football husk and creek—can't. It needs you. What you want, you have. What you have, you've conjured. What you add, you take away. The lowering shadows, hot-fleshed jogger on the beamless little bridge. Trying to fit yourself in, and ten thousand miles from the truth.

Dark-green pine tree, bright-green field. No—green pine, green grass. Pine, grass. No—skinny needles. Sticks. Things. Blades. Not-this, not-that. Trillium. No—white petal. Petal. White. How white? How petal? Why not? Originally there's no rattle, no scrounge, no scatter, no settle, no jagged, no rippling wave. The tension pulls you between the leaf moving on its own and the leaf compelled to move by the wind, rejecting all adjectives, verbs, adverbs. Call the bush yellow, the stalks rose, the needles sharp, and instantly they aren't. They're: "yellow, rose, sharp." Whatever mood you're in, whatever dim memories flicker on the fire, the way you were caught on a rose bush as a child outside your neighbour's deadbolted door. A shrill whip of cold, the bloody streaks, your weeping. Not-this. Not-that.

I want to scoop out my eyes and put things back in without the need for other things. I want to look and see directly. I want to bring my questions to the bark of a tree and ask in another language. I cannot say what

I mean. If I make everything happen, what makes me make it happen? If the leaf moves not by wind but by mind, then what makes mind? Ask the pine? How do I stop the plastic feeling? The grey, spongy turf and the wide ruin? The turning to you, spell I've summoned, and telling you how marvellous the rabbits look in the sunset, haloed by the dying dandelions, shivering into the air and into memory? To stop turning to you to make it new—not-this, not-that—and merely vibrate in my lonesome admiration, here, while the earth is warm and sweet?

# "AME NI MO MAKEZU"

*In tribute to Kenji Miyazawa (1896–1933)*

I CAN WITHSTAND the rain, whipping me in greasy strips, as I'm launched off the bus and out, limpy, toward a job for the 409th day. I can rebuff the wind, its cocktail of toxins from Coco Paving, the vomitorium where cement gets made, and a steel recycling centre that screams at 2:00 p.m. exactly. I am immune to the snow in my faux-leather boots and to the trickle of sweat down my Jockeys in August—safe from it all, manufactured, nitrous oxide, particles of heaven. My body is strong from Vega One, dog walks, and DDP Yoga. My desires spill out in short webs of excitement and are instantly forgotten, flushing budding lives from a Bardo into one endless toilet bowl, and I flagellate myself with bone-white earbuds should I recall a juvenile ambition. I whisper a half-held "hi" into the bog-green lockers and slip in "sorry" and "thank you" interchangeably, to interchangeable call-centre kids, doing what I call the Chump Face, which is kind of a smile, kind of a grimace, and every day I make a rich and complicated salad for my desktop lunch, eat oats and fruit for breakfast. I board the late bus last, always, and stand when seats are at a premium, perform breathing exercises to conjure a species of love even for the cretins blocking the crush and the howling faces in the back. I watch and listen to nineteen YouTube videos a day and never once lose my composure. Sometimes it's people-parks where Brazilian jiu-jitsu boys burn small pyres of garbage; sometimes we do dog parks where men sip cold Americanos and women dress down, big time; and sometimes the steel railpaths and rivers of Toronto float before us in a mini-hurricane vision that churns up Loose Meat. Above us, in the rental, furious workmen clobber the floors, and splinters rise like chilled hair, electric goose, while the carpet rots with mould and bossy kids get their wet reward under the daily bloom of renovation, houses demolished and rebuilt, refurbished for people who are fathomlessly rich. Spying out a tiny office window at the children dancing, playing Cherry Bomb in the grassy circle, fighting, defining rules and calling fouls that require a wail to resolve. Silently, alone behind the marbled glass, I pull a Chump Face. If one of these babies is sick and shrieks to join its lispy friends, raging in its mother's grasp, I wince. If Mom is tired, I pity her, thinking I could shoulder her bag of artisanal cheese and diapers if only she'd let me. And when the ambulance slides into view without dreadful march or stern alarum to pick the dying olds from their homes like hunks of grass-fed beef from our boulevard's jaw, I say, there is no need to be afraid, dear chest-wracked lady in these endgame pajamas, and whisper a half-remembered prayer about wishing her next life is a good one, and not what I secretly hope for—a centipede. Quarrels rage on social; my old friends sue new friends; the defamed sue accusers; the people hold opinions with tensile strength; and I pour an entire bottle of shiraz down the sink while wearing grey boxer briefs. When the romaine lettuce gets all fucked with salmonella, we buy iceberg instead. When the summer never heats up but keeps the chill of early spring, hey, it's all we talk about as we buy perfumed candles, pretend to work, donate blood, ride the dry buses, bump into our seething neighbours, stare into the sky's pit, or wander far from home at night to Our Guy at 7-Eleven to buy a secret pack of Pall Malls, hoping to run into someone new. When you're outside the gastropub, you're a nobody; if the night's clearly over but you keep roaming, drunk, in your leather daddy jacket, you can't be blamed. And if the years trickle on without promotion or demotion but whoa, you're still employed, then it's still a paycheque, which is more than we can say for those living in the next province or tent-based prefecture. Better than the next life—please god! Please, to all the gods of the six realms meeting here between my pressed palms: this is the type of person I want to become.

# HYPOAROUSAL

IMAGINE THE FOLLOWING dream: you're walking across a thin, rope-strung bridge spanning a bottomless, foggy chasm. You are alone in a cold, pastel, coniferous wilderness, a waterfall roaring somewhere nearby. And there, materializing out of the draping mist two hundred feet ahead, along the same precarious rope-strung bridge, is your worst enemy—the profile you might imagine when I say, "Picture your least favourite person." There is nowhere to escape, no thoughts of avoiding them as they stride confidently toward you. Imagine your dream telling you, "Oh, this person is my greatest enemy," and feeling a lance of panic and fear.

Imagine dreaming that you couldn't wake up from your life, or you couldn't fundamentally change or escape your life, or that you had to be alive today and tomorrow and tomorrow and for another hundred years in this current situation, as if it were a sentence, with circumstances gradually becoming worse for you hour by hour. Imagine that even suicide was impossible; that you had to stay right here, where you are, in this very logical, consistent, and coherent dream.

Imagine dreaming of a Facebook post that's not about you, written by someone who doesn't know you and never will, written about something you are not remotely related to or responsible for, and yet feeling so attacked and shamed by it that your morning and afternoon and weekend are ruined, and you spend days of your dream imagining rebuttals and coded responses that could lob back a retort smart enough to make this person, this shadowy something online who doesn't know you and never will, feel an agonizing wound open in their heart.

Imagine dreaming that there was a kind of truth in books or movies or television or paintings or music or dance—a truth in art, however you define or despise or celebrate it—that could unspool the riddle of your dreams and add up, accumulate, aggregate, expand upon you, make you better than whatever you are now, and dispel the yawning jaw of the next several decades, which you will spend watching the people you love get sick and die with dread and hate steadily uncoiling in their minds.

Imagine dreaming that the countless therapies, medications, meditations, treatments, and spiritual systems invented over thousands of years simply didn't work for you; that the remedies invented to counter your exact combination of anxiety and despair were somehow designed for other people only—that your unique human mind was and is the sole exception among all other human minds and the ways they've marched out of hell. That in this particular dream, you are unworthy of salvation.

Imagine dreaming that time truly did exist; that the energy that has taken you out of figure skating or Little League T-ball and orange slices or Girl Guides and dodgeball or your dorm room or that melodramatic first heartbreak in perfectly congruent December rain was actually linear, a process of cause and effect—a sequence of events, with one thing leading to another, creating a past, present, and future, trapping you in its river, its ineluctable churn, and binding you to a knowledge of impending old age, sickness, death—and that you are already at least halfway through the process of one thing happening, then another thing, then another thing, all traced by a ribbon, until nothing, nothing mattering at all.

Imagine a dream in which your body and all surrounding matter were solid and actually there, real, discrete; glass panes firm, steel unyielding, flesh and bone impenetrable, and even air made up of blocks of various thicknesses and forms; that you were a lump, a distinction with angles and mass. Nothing more than that, and nothing less. No wonder you're worried about cuts and bruises, a burnt throat from bile, an abscessed tooth! No wonder the dream creates a sense of desperate uncertainty about your well-being, the gurgle of your guts or the weird twitches of your eyelid, bodily harms gathering in dramatic ensemble. The world a baseball bat, your head a pumpkin, and you nothing but the sum of the seeds, the shell, and a cruel geometry.

Imagine dreaming of another person's success and praise, and regardless of how deserving they are, and regardless of how undeserving you are of anything close to the exact terms of praise this person is receiving, you nevertheless feel such an intense jealousy and righteous self-pity that you begin to besmirch and discredit or fail to support this person—the recipient of praise from others—in dozens of small, semi-conscious ways while simultaneously wanting this person to meet you and get to know you and soon, finally, shower you with their own affections, which heretofore have yet to be tasted.

Imagine dreaming that depression was a necessary part of being a creative person. In this dream you resign yourself to your depression; you post about it, joke about it, wallow in it, commiserate about it, and become deeply suspicious of all methods of solving or relieving it, especially if those methods involve reorganizing how you perceive the world in a metaphysical or epistemological sense, and especially if they challenge this long-held belief about yourself: that your creativity, your artistic constitution, the arched brow with which you view the busy material fretting of the world—eyes that are slits of suspicion but nostrils flared by the undeniable bouquet of savage beauty attending all this urgent activity—came at the cost of your general day-to-day happiness, and could only be relieved by what, more creativity? Some big daddy or mommy, back from the dead to say you are good? A hug? A red-carpet gala? Your name stitched across a billboard of stars for your collection of short stories, which we all agreed was pretty good?

Imagine dreaming about a glistening, taffeta-white 2018 Honda Civic shivering by in the damp evening mist, still trailing tendrils of moisture from the first dream about your worst enemy approaching along a rope-strung bridge. Imagine dreaming about its hazy taillights and how, simply by their similarity to a different scene you experienced twenty years ago, they trigger a long-buried memory of adolescent grief: the cat put to sleep while you were merrily off at swimming lessons. Imagine dreaming of a passenger jet winking in the stars above and being chased by a meteor. Imagine dreaming of seasons passing, of infographics detailing fossil fuel emissions, of sheepdogs shaking off mud, of a heart-shaped circle of poplar trees, of an orb spider named Norman in your grandfather's mason jar, and believing they were permanent things—objects of form that existed independently, animals that lived and loved and died independently of this dream, frittering on into futures not requiring you to dream them into being this very moment. Where were we? An ancient stab of grief. Your parents breaking the news about Rory the tabby while you were out swimming like a schmuck. *Oh, I was sad*, you think, watching the Honda Civic slip away. And then imagine: you actually become sad!

"I want to wake up, I want to wake up," you say in another dream, and make a pathetic noise. I want to experience the indescribable surety I feel knowing the dream, which had seemed entirely real to me just moments earlier, has slipped away into non-existence, and that I have returned to a place that is not a dream, which I call wakefulness, with its rich and often boring patina of possibilities, its signature pains and consistent unease shooting through everything I am, only because I know I can wake up, that there is another pain possible, that I can look behind me at the dream I thought was real and say, "Oh, I understand now, I am awake, and all that is over."

# SANDŌKAI, NON-BINARY

*In tribute to Shítóu Xīqiān (700–790)*

NO MATTER ON TikTok or Twitch, a great mind—say a sage, say an Adderall brain—conveys itself like an embedded system: universal Wi-Fi and the Internet of Things. It enfolds the Musks and Dorseys, the wireframes for Discord, as close as the breath in the mouth: the word *abba* sung in Aramaic by Christ. The Kingdom of Heaven, the Other Shore, Baidu Incorporated—nothing to win or work toward. And though we follow simps and cucks, NPCs, Susans, normies, and yes—hot girls, doomers, and the woke—such intimacy gives zero fucks about a God or a daddy, 5G networks or dial-ups made of smoke.

"The subtle source is clear and bright." Free Getty images of the earth at night showcase streams of light clustered to places where we grimace in darkness. In the last watch of the evening, the sun remains as furious, burning for the next five billion years of boredom. Born, just respawned, and already a room of things arrayed for me: Wayfair crib, Walmart mobiles, Amazon nappies, and plush facsimiles of extinction-bound Cetacea from the WWF, which I clutch in terror. Later, the cataract: I learned to be a wonk, then a monk, wadding it all together, but this only compounded my problem. How I discriminate, following some, not others; thinking Ivy League or HVAC; being strict about being non-binary. Being OCD about oblivion. How I learned to write a bio rattling off my POV.

Without you there is no social network, and yet the social network scrolls on without compassion in your wake. Deeper: the realization that all laws are power, arbitrary, and yet the need for laws arises even as we defund the police. Deeper, oh Gamer Girl, the experience of seeing and the Oculus lens are different and none other than the same: codependent, independent, emotional labour, yes honey when it's four o'clock and time for one's dick to be flattened by one's Trad Girl semblance. There was a definite UX but there is also no UX at all—you can no longer connect to the server, and even the Wayback Machine turns up void. What happened is now past, and the past does not exist, so it never happened. Nothing happens, full stop. And yet our memories of dial-up are conveyed intimately, like the Great Mind of India.

The aesthetic lurks in every user; everyone's a critic. Everyone has a Spotify Top Ten, and people have style, religious convictions. I enjoy novels that win the Giller. Cardi B is both pure and unclean, depending on the darkness visible. The K-pop, the drone screams, the eight-lane highway. A hierarchy. Falling asleep, sounds become doom-jazz-ambient; when awake, voices determine happiness and class. There is little to determine Mariah Carey's larynx from yours but oh what a difference an octave makes at Christmas. Eyes closed and the realm of sight departs; ears plugged and all we hear is ocean; mouth shuts and wisdom takes root. Eventually, this fun-sized animated bobble—once a baby with a Walmart mobile, a stuffed whale in bullied fist—reverts to its constituents: water, vapour, heat, solids. Rain and sewer grates. A landfill of e-waste, ready to be recycled, and gulls circling storm clouds on wings of shit.

"A child turns to its mother." Of course! Naturally, a child without a mother is no child at all. A child-sized casket exists because the child once lived. No child, no container; no fetus, no growing womb. In "Heart-Shaped Box," a song about vaginas, Cobain sings of the umbilical noose, of "climbing right back." Stripped of metaphor, wombs are wet, blood is warm, bones are white, and the baby's breath is sweet. Baby's breath, the thing the nose smells, so the nose itself is baby's breath, and still not quite a nose—just intimately fitted, through contact and feeling, like a mobile getting tangled in its self-created current; like a lid snapped shut on a heart-shaped coffin. Imagine blaming the baby's breath on the nose. Imagine tweeting about it, getting five thousand retweets, then killing yourself after a flood of hate drowns your DMs. As such, the normies live, setting up standards, like their front and back sneaks never meet.

Do not waste your time. I'm begging you, like the men who exhort me daily to put aside childish things, to make my bed and clean my room. But one more podcast clip or press junket, one more anti-vaxxer thread unspooled, another .png swiped right—another block in my Minecraft mountain, my Discord confession to zero contacts, endless twilight. But inside those blocks, a great mind—even blocks we build ourselves. Even the vilest tongue on Twitch confesses mystery; even Logan and Jake Paul refract a darkness that makes the world one. Do not waste your time chasing tendrils or subreddits; do not ignore the roots beneath the tree. Don't get trapped like a critic in *The Walrus*, guessing far and wee, calling it objective, making mountains sprout and rivers roar—doomed to be a loser for this life and the next.

# ME FIRST

HOW IS IT that I create social isolation in senior populations? How do I provoke the angry cat that swats the woolen elves from the mantlepiece, or a man's reluctant viewing of *The Last Jedi*? It's me who summons a photo of Jewish refugees from 1946, me who summons their tinned winces, the long draught of hunger, but what I'm asking is how: how do I create someone else's PTSD from childhood neglect? How at once do I contrive a favourite queer writer of 2019 and flail, helplessly, to do anything else? How do I also create a review of *Cats* (2019) and a framing device around the film and someone else's endorsement of both the device and the original review and never watch the film beginning to end? Tell me! Without effort, how do I complot the frustration I feel with the popular TERF message board and the conventionally attractive white woman posting on the board, creating both her symmetrical face in her profile picture and my judgment of her politics? How do I make the .gif of the diapered babies slapping each other in the upper-middle-class kitchen and my surety that this .gif was shared by someone who does not understand the internet? Yes, I create the tinge of snot and the urge to wipe with the ball of TP. I make the dry, bitten lip and the curled bloodline, even the battery taste of puke. I call forth my disgust with the joke about weight, the times people eat, types of food people eat, how much or how little they are eating, and how fat they feel. I make all my sorrows line up neatly in the morning, still a stinky poo in bed, which I created from something called the field of possibility, which is always empty and which I am invited to ponder, to be aware of in awe or in endless cycles of diapers and all that gross debt. Sorrows that are uninvited, patient, gather around my creaky mattress like transparent ghosts, no more present than the fact of the plaster, the bedsheets, my love's sleeping breath, or the ragged glob of sunlight lashed to the wall, reminding me that the reason my friend Daniela no longer invites me to parties is because I got too drunk at her house once and threw up on the cab ride home. I manufacture the fear when scrolling through outback firestorms, all those crispy koalas, feel despondent yet privileged to watch The End, and invent ways to provide comfort to my neighbours rotting from fallout instead of hoarding cans of Chunky Chicken Corn Chowder in my cannibal, COVID basement. I make my outrage at free speech absolutists and I make my outrage about perceived censorship. I make the 11:00 a.m. sunlight on the yellow brick wall in the alley behind our shared hovel and the shadow of the ornaments, the bitter cold and the wakeful caffeinated slurpee of joy, the rumble of capitalist Christmas radio from Bing Crosby and the squeal of the upstairs espresso machine. I made my admiration for Brittany Murphy and filled (filled!) the dearth of critical commentary on her luminous career with my own shady way of thinking. I assembled my jealousy of my colleague's achievement award while inventing the award and the hairs on his chin and his incessant mumble-humming anxiety. I invent the jubilation of tax work going well, a hooded youth lurking alongside a Lexus and surreptitiously trying the handle, ruined hands worked raw from homeless weather, and the reason I no longer hear from my friend Cynthia: because of a joke I made that she perceived as a slight that went untriaged for months, then years, and now lives beneath a scab that hurts for always, and only in my imagination, which also houses Jupiter, for example, and Ganymede, and Hollywood Boulevard. That every slurp of soup from the poriferous man in the louche café while I work on my fraudulent resumé has bided its time until these perfect, present conditions, and is now blooming like a regal geranium in my one and only universe. But how, is what I'm asking.

# LATE CAPITALISM

THE MIND IS simply magical! Lowell J. Propriety of Valiant Pharmaceuticals is on a stake. I mean, some buff red demon with a wicked top-knot picked him up, flipped him upside down, and shoved him (mouth-first!) onto a sharpened ten-foot spear, which was forced through his body and out his butt, and there he hangs, living still, choking on the wood. Valiant's former CEO, Mickey Righteousness, is beside him in the exact same predicament, except sometimes he passes out from the pain. Mr. Bluebell Integrity of Magnanimous International was lowered lovingly into a dank tub of boiling cum, allowed to soften up, and then was flayed, living; his skin was then used as mummy rags for Stetson "The Hammer" Shame, former president and CEO of Obedience, Determination and Associates (ODA). Stetson is forced to suffocate to death in a different robe of Bluebell's wet skin every night. The former president and CEO of Reliable Communications, Vanilla B. Loyalty, has his eyes removed by another buff (but this time bright blue!) demon every morning, added to a kind of suss collection plate, then eaten by an enormous vulture. Vanilla's shitty eyes regrow, slowly and extremely painfully, through a night of crawling through scabland and rot. Can you imagine how Perfecto Piety III, the CEO of Canadian Politeness Railway, screamed as rats chewed their way through the wound, severed by blunt garden shears, where his tiny dick and distended balls used to be? They made it right through his bowels and into his guts before they ate each other and died. Chadfield Benevolence was the CEO of Tranquil Responsibility Corp., but now he's wrapped around a white-hot metal rod, which sizzles and blisters his skin like the bacon strips he once liked to gobble. And Billyjack Love's tongue is in Mathdaniel Honesty's mouth and sewn in there; Mathdaniel's cock has been in Billyjack's colon for eons; they've swapped limbs and digits and are sewn face-to-face (Mr. Love was CEO of Frugal Industries and Mr. Honesty the CEO of Equanimity Corp.). Kermit Ikea Justice, CEO of Cleanliness Connections, is sealed in a coffin full of monstrous tarantulas and eaten alive every forty-five minutes; and this will continue long enough for a boulder to be rubbed away by the silk caress of a Harry Rosen bow tie. But here we have a Tigerlily star-wipe: the mind is magical, okay? It invents ferns and summer skies, orgasms and hurt feelings, your mother's face when she was still young and inexpressibly beautiful, but you never told her, did you? And all within the flutter of an oak leaf, or a pool noodle. Ha! Swipes of ultraviolet, then living coral, then back to our feature presentation: Adonis Harmony of Meekness Financial Corp. is trapped (or, more accurately, impaled) in a tree made of swords—speaking of magic—while the CEO of Curiosity Corp., Kati Smoki-Peace, recipient of over \$14,640,000 in compensation, has her ass eaten, literally, by a hangry dire wolf beside the tree's jagged roots (and did you see Dr. Infinite Faith, Chairman of the same company, recipient of nearly \$12,000,000 in compensation, be digested alive by the same legendary Ass-Hound? Because I did!). Below Kati is the sad case of Seaborn Beanbag Morality, who was lodged into an iceberg, whose flesh is as midnight blue as a hunk of meat left in a freezer, with all those classic freezer-burn fronds. But he can feel everything, immobile in his suffering for as long as his former employer, Cleanliness Connections, can have its terrifically bad deeds worked out by time and habit, up into space and starlight. Likewise, Hannah Hearkening of Solidarity Corp. has been reduced to an urn of grue and gristly body parts—arms and entrails and wet silver-pocked molars—but she'll still blink up at you in misery as you march past, locked into your own buzz. Who's in charge down here, she seems to plead with those glistening peepers, as Decoldest Charity of the Bank of Critical Thinking and Barron Wisdom of the Royal Bank of Forgiveness get nailed together in the nude, back to back, with a feathered javelin thrust through their well-fed torsos. Yes, magic! But why? Why is the world so filled with sorcery? Who decides, who gets to cast these unbearable spells? Why were we born naked into the world, shoved naked and ill-favoured into a ditch, and on the way, lose everything we love, only to end up here, ruined, with these fabulous thought leaders? Mouth full of blood for the poor souls in endless arrears! Mouth full of blood here erasing my browser history! Mouth full of blood and my silk bow tie slowly rubbing down a boulder, waiting to update my portfolio, waiting for the world to be gentle, to volunteer for someone else's pain.

II

# APERTURE II

EVERY NOW AND then I see the fern shaking and see the fern shaking. Eyes, generally, grew accidentally as we flung off our single-celled histories, yet the transcendental experience often involves another way of seeing. Veils are stripped. Scales fall away. Luckily, both Saul and Mr. Potato Head have their pupils, and irises, and long buxom lashes, and explore a range of luminous flux. Everything is exactly as it is, but you are not. How wonderful to pierce the dark by simply blinking. The fern shaking. The round, white butterfly a thaumatrope on the deck. Gilmour Avenue, blowing summer. The horse galloping on the roll of film is not galloping—it is a series of photographs of a horse. Your eye and the zoetrope of the fern. Nothing moving. Nothing can move.

And yet, I thought, in the ecstasy of my conversion, tears soaking my four-dollar T-shirt, of a soap bubble. I would never know the edge of the veil. I was trapped, wonderfully, inside this bubble: a turbaned boy at the bottom of the Arabian, a Djinni's plaything. My eyes could see only what they could see, up to the limits of vision, so nothing could harm me. I cried because ... I was safe, finally. I was the warm cabin in the mountains ringed by the baying of wolves. I was the steel cage in the ocean, sharks of the mind inhaling chum just outside the bars. I did not have to be a good boy—no more, you fakes, you maniacs! I could sit down, here, anywhere, in the bubble, and let my projects drop, all at once, like scales falling from tiny paper eyes.

There is another way, a clearer way, to see the fern shaking and see the fern shaking and it is to see the fern as a product and blessing of your vision, which occurs for you only; and the limits of vision are themselves a clever way to signal that there is no fern outside you, for there it is, shaking, ultimately still, within the boundaries of your eye. That there are boundaries should in turn signal that you are everything that is. What else could be outside the boundaries? Nothing, an impossibility to experience, and yet all our problems impale us from the imaginary outside. Hailing, like incorrigible wrestling heels, from parts unknown—tearing through the curtain and into the light. Where were you before you were born: a ghost story. Where were you after you died: a haunting. The gnashing jaws of others, forming their terrible opinions.

We have always been in the womb; we never left. When Venus pierces the veil of night she shines as an afterimage, a revolving wheel, yet this eye is not a camera, and yet you alone are. You alone, and yet you are not a cynic, and not a narcissist, and not a solipsist. You are the world's one and only honoured thing and thus the world—the fern does not shake—and yet the tears slipped from your eyes and onto your cheeks and into your cheap cotton. Other people come up the trail and cross your borders. They wave to you, bring you great comfort in your solitude: bowls of rice, pails of water, grass sandals, the occasional letter from someone far away. They slip between the soapy veil of the very edge of what you can see and suddenly they're inside you, holding you, rocking you, teaching you, arousing in you a pity so wide and so deep it's enough to keep looking for an eye long after your sockets hold only water, and you are wandering on again, groping for light.

# REASONS FOR MY SUCCESS

I WAS NOT nice. I was not nice enough. I was not nice enough to the right people. My niceness was too casual; my niceness was designed for acquaintances and so it had no lasting impact. I carried out acts of niceness too long ago for people to remember today, and too long ago for those distributing acts of niceness now. I forgot the intention behind my niceness and so grew weary of niceness in all its forms. I was not nice consistently, or deliberately, in public, and so withdrew my general, fit-for-acquaintances-style niceness, a quality ready for all comers, to a shrinking circle of people I really did care about, for whom I could maintain the energy required of niceness, and for whom my niceness changed its character, becoming intimate, or something else not quite nice at all. My acts of niceness were spotty. When I attempted acts of niceness in public I felt strange and inauthentic with increasing intensity. My acts of niceness cowed me: I felt hot and ashamed for my expressions of niceness, especially when these expressions were not acknowledged by their recipients. I felt expressing niceness made the objects of my niceness uncomfortable, occasionally, or made these people for whom I was expressing niceness turn against me and categorize me as "not nice." The people for whom I performed niceness were the wrong people, insofar as they are no longer in positions to perform public acts of reciprocal niceness; or they are not accustomed to expressing private acts of niceness; or they feel no need to reciprocate niceness, at least not to me, or to those like me, to people in my predicament. I failed to understand that I was not and am not deserving of niceness, per se or period. I failed to account for all the terrible things I said out loud and in private, often while intoxicated and happy, thinking I was sharing niceness—for the wasted years of my life when being nice was of fundamental importance. My acts of niceness, no longer public or consistent, made others believe I did not wish to receive acts of niceness myself: that I was somehow above or uninterested in public acts of niceness, when in truth I craved them desperately. I was furthermore not nice in sufficient public and private ways to people who interpreted my niceness to certain distasteful people as problematic. I was nice to people who are today irrelevant to public consideration; I was also nice to people who are not fit recipients for public niceness, to whom extending niceness was an ethical breach, or a sign that my niceness was too fluid or generous, despite my niceness being merely of a casual, passing nature, as mentioned. I was not nice enough to people who believe niceness must be parceled out judiciously to those who, by fact of their relationship or discipline or social standing, are more deserving of public or private acts of niceness than others, regardless of the overall volume of niceness being expressed. I was not nice enough to those who, through some history of being hurt or abused, considered their own niceness a limited resource. I failed to be eligible to receive niceness from those who feel acts of niceness are made primarily for public consumption, on momentous occasions, and for a select group only. I was, paradoxically, too nice to make a fuss about those who were not nice, to me or to others with whom I held acquaintance or even friendship. I failed to reveal my private sense of injustice or hypocrisy, cruelty or betrayal in a public setting, and thus was categorized as someone who was "not nice" (though less "not nice" than if I had expressed the full storm of my emotional life, as then I would have been "not nice" to a much more damaging, irreparable extent). And I failed to grasp how others could be nice in public to people they deemed "problematic" or "not nice" or insufficiently deserving in private, and thus I refrained from expressing niceness to those by whom I was betrayed, systematically. I failed to grasp that acts of niceness made in person are of lesser quality than public acts of niceness made from a great distance, and with far less intimacy. My niceness had limitations fit to my disposition and imaginary sense of self-worth. I failed to sustain the energy necessary for daily, weekly acts of niceness due to my body's aging, that stated sense of inauthenticity, a general weariness borne of failed applications and unnumbered rejections, the demands of dull and pitiless work, and the emptiness of public gestures. Resigning myself to not being nice, or being deemed "not nice," or not especially deserving of niceness, felt nice, bizarrely, but only for a few months, after which I again felt it would be nice to feel included in the worldly, public exchange of niceness, but by then it was too late to re-enter with the same enthusiasm or trust I had felt when younger and less experienced with the vagaries of being nice. To measure my lack of suitability to receive niceness from others, I compiled a voluminous list of every person with whom I'd shared an acquaintance, correspondence, and/or friendship, then wrote three to seven reasons beside each, in sharp bullet points, why each person might not be nice to me, why they would not extend niceness to me, and why I might deserve this withholding of niceness. This list included those who were closest to me, those who had extended niceness to me in the past and why they had stopped doing so, and those who had never expressed niceness to me in the first place and why that was the case and would continue to be so. The work of this list was decidedly "not nice," loaded with shameful revelations and remembrances, though it felt nice in the same way a spanking feels nice, or a candlelit confession, or chores or a punishment or a sentence; the way a failing grade feels nice, or a reprimand at work; the way a traffic ticket or a dressing down by a superior feels nice. But it did not stop me from trying to think of newer, nicer things I could do for people to vindicate myself in their eyes and be the subject, or object, of nice expressions once again. Where I was headed with this list was a concrete feeling of "not niceness" in my chest and a "not nice" urge to sob. This list became my vocation, my sole hobby, which replaced my older hobbies and vocational activities that were, to my chagrin, bound up in dense, complex feelings of equilibrium, fairness, and withheld niceness, and so charged my nights, after my "not nice" work was finished, with a sense of purpose and clarity, a lack of generalized guilt and a new sterling specificity regarding the shame I felt about myself and my failure to express niceness in adequate degree, quality, or frequency. Using my list, and knowing deeply this was folly, I embarked on long campaigns of niceness, whereby regardless of how it made me feel hollow or aggrieved, confused or impotent, I wrote relentless nice messages to people and performed niceness in public spaces, hoping these unrequested acts would cleanse my spleen and my remorse, my antipathy and aversion, but they did not, for they burnt up like smoke, so to speak, cycling skyward to form billows that were instead, rather than recognizable in shape (as if emanating from any conscious mind or designer), incomprehensible, chaotic; neither nice nor "not nice" but merely neutral, drifting wisps of vapour, empty of content or memory; clear and lovely as a glass held up to clouds filled with rain.

# HANDS AND EYES

### After Hekiganroku, Case 89

*for Steph*

THE DOG IS thirsty, so we let it drink; we pour cold water into its tin
bowl and watch its eyes close in pleasure as the water soothes its throat. It
doesn't know we gave it the bowl; it knows only this pleasure, and I'm in
a black pool beside it, watching the body with hands and eyes. We found
a nest of blackbirds in a steel electrical pole in the crucifix of August,
begging at a thin strip of air. Their mother circled and wailed above us and
didn't know it had laid its diamonds in an oven. We pried a metal plate off
the pole in scandalous daylight, using our rusted, second-hand tools, trying
to give them a breeze, a relief, while men ripped donuts around us on quad
bikes. And success—the birds would live until nightfall; the babies would
eat. We had made that happen, conspiring with the metal, watching the
weight of the hammers, caressing the birds with the knotty little muscles
in our eyes. Moving through the one body of this life, all at once, slapped

awake, or bled slowly, exhausted by an arrow piercing our hide as we pant and tire through a neon wood, we come to know that everything is on fire. The endless ambulances bleeding down to the overpass; the grackles and sparrows announcing it's morning; the marimba ringtones ushering us to hated, wretched work: I'm on fire. Please. I'm on fire!

You make a list. The possum writhing with flies, flesh eaten as it spasmed, that we squatted over in July, fanning it, hushing it, until it stopped. The dog who lived and dreamed his long life beneath the rusted pick-up truck in Belarus. The rabbit who found its last sibling to lie and die beside, bodies stricken with disease, in the glory of our backyard, all through one eternal weekend. The grubs cut in two by our needling shovels. The fruit flies foundering in a warm glass of wine. The sow hung by its dainty feet and then torched, living, to blister off its divinity. You, sitting with a pain in your hip, an unanswered email triggering a typhoon of abandonment. Last night I dreamt of a crow on fire, burning to death. Then I lay awake in bed, trying to perceive the point. What was the lesson? I imagined many fabulous distractions: having one thousand eyes to caress; having one thousand hands to witness. I imagined the crow that suffered and died could take medicine from my mind, make a meal of my bowels, drink the rivers of my blood, wear my hair when it's winter. I imagined it could use my tongue to say it hurts, it hurts, and I would be there, saying, my baby, I'm burning, too! I'm on fire just like you are. And saying: moving through the body is hands and eyes. Saying, there is only hands and eyes.

# THE CHAOS MAGICIAN

THE FIRST PERSON to pick up their phone loses and also wins big. That's a dream I had. That's a cold open; that's a child of a bad script. I'm a recreational consequence, getting a rebate on experiential hormones, paying someone plastic to rehydrate me on King Street. We are getting an apartment visit from a Chaos Magician: a man who wields a cleansing penis. He went to the University of Consciousness for a part-time program in phone circles and content contamination, now gets wasted on painkillers and vodka and makes wild, eternal children to overpopulate *The Last of Us* via Zappos and Pets.com. It stemmed from a Chipotle incident in the Stockyards, when I tapped my Visa on the wet spot, a left-of-centre decision to remain disembodied that prompted strange side effects, like *The Doctors*, *Dr. Oz*, *The Social*, and the precise time of 3:08 p.m., CP24, in the middle of a shit winter. The Chaos Magician gives a grim prognosis: BAD LANGUAGE. The Chaos Magician gives expensive advice. He tells me the more I bleach the toilet the more I will know the toilet is an altar, a puja or a butsudan; that the more I masturbate the more I will want to masturbate, so I should start masturbating right away, even though I must realize I will be at the very first primary level and there are ninety-nine levels, each with its own payment plan. His consumers are more like superfans, you understand, who help construct community around his brand. *Ask yourself,* he asks. *How much do you want to inhabit the product world? How much do you want to evangelize or self-identify with the product world?* There are niche subsets of right-of-centre rationalist communities clustering up around masochism, excessive self-care, "nailing it," and *Parasite*; wealth apps, ramen noodle museums, colon cancer, *Paris Spleen*, and old wailing melancholy—a wound that is so cute. These are his words, not mine. The Chaos Magician. *So angry,* he says. *What are you going to do with all that anger? You think "things" make you angry, but it comes from up here*—and he knocks on your skull. You ball up your hands into fists and smash your ergonomic keyboard to pieces like some goddamned gorilla. You shaved your eyebrows and tattooed the names of your MMO allies there instead in tiny, Satanic script (the first one says "headshot," the next says "pwned" and the next spells out three hundred names of God and the next one says "PewDiePie" and the next one is the name of the hamster you poked with a pen in grade 3 and the next one says "RITUAL"). Ellen Degeneres gets it, or nails it, but *Funny or Die* doesn't. This quote from Peter Capaldi totally nails the appeal of *Doctor Who*. Green Day's biggest fan joins them on stage and totally nails it. A toddler totally nails the Water Bottle Challenge and the standing ovation gave me real chills. The standing ovation for the toddler granted me a secret empowerment meant for a select elite. The Chaos Magician interrogates me, gaslights me, drags my ass to the teapot, and asks in discrete micro-aggressions if I know the heiress angle, the e-girl scandal; if I own an eco-friendly Ouija board to conjure the American waterfront grocery store while two Leonards discuss xennial dads. Do I know that a group of liberals is called an airstrike? Bad Language. Do I know that a group of conservatives is called more airstrikes? Bad Language. Rituals nearing completion, my name, it turns out, is Robotics; my name is "nice person." So, cremation for me, says our visitor; SWAT teams and random frisks, recruited through social ads on TikTok that ask, in .mp4 and poor lip-reads, how much I could make working from home—as a registered nurse who makes plastic friendship bracelets, as an expat who tweaks meditation apps to help dogs sleep, or as a vape-shop girl who twists lip-gloss containers that say "Unconscious Yet Consciously Sexy." More cocaine, more cocaine for us. Iced up jeeps, rented Lamborghinis for us. Still, the ghosts have departed—yep, got it, check—at least the ectos are gone! The ghosts have been put to sleep in a rear-naked choke, the halogens no longer flicker all poltergeisty, and I certainly do not dream. I do not dream, do not dream; that played-out Bardo would upset the tender stem of the single rose rotting in a saucer in the company kitchen, and if disturbed, would fully explode my myths. *I'm a sad white dude full of shit*, says the Chaos Magician, now fucking my pony-shaped tulpa with his wisping penis, his crown of thorns and vinous cologne. You're an introvert sadly slouching toward extroversion. We've a boundless capacity to cast shade on the empty shades now rattling the rafters, all wearing aviators of serenity blue and rose quartz that make it seem like 2016 never went poof, up in autism. Bro, the blood bags never dried! Bro, we never cried, "Cheeto Man Bad!" Bro, your best friends are immortal, manga—your best friends do not die alone with foregone funerals to service the rapidly changing situation in the Metro and the LCBO, where we stay apart to stay close. Bro, you are not dreaming. And yet here you are, you putz, you fraud, you Vulnerable Narcissist—making your Divine Judgment on my Christina Aguilera, "Dirty"-era mess. *Bad Language*, he says. *Bad Language is to blame for all of this*. So we broke his limbs and hung him on a cross and burnt him to death on West Queen West.

# CADETS-IN-TRAINING PRESENTATION, TORONTO POLICE COLLEGE, 2020

"SOMEONE WAS ASKING earlier about creation and personal responsibility. About my comments on one mind and body. In particular, how we create the suspect—the potential suspect, the to-be-determined suspect—sidling up to the Lexus. We have a few more minutes, so …"

He pauses, blinking in the dust-filled glare of the projector, the white beam in the Aegean classroom. Someone coughs.

"You create the suspect through eye and ear—its particular gait and fricatives, its melanin and gaze. A host of formal etceteras: colour, sound, shape. So use your generous benefits packages. Without healthy cartilage or gelatin there's no perception. I mean, no feelings of vesture and illustrator, emblem, or affect. No perceptions of naming, a sobriquet, a call sign or nomenclature, simple demonym of recognition. Yes? And no formative process of discernment—no flying toward the suspect, like iron ore to a magnet; no contact-making in every arising now. The nose, too: odour of terpene, skunk, sweetness on the breath. Leading one to deduce. Though we don't suggest a tongue bath, there are flavours on the air that reward processing. Bitterness, for one."

A desk scrapes. Weight settles as a creak, a winch, in a chair. Fingers clack against a plastic keyboard.

"When I look up at the subject in the streetlight, what I want to realize acutely is that this looking is its own event; this looking, in this hypothetical arising present, has never happened previously. It cannot happen again, even in a *Groundhog Day* scenario. Another look is a different looking because at the very least I am renewed entirely. And it exists for one consciousness, period. The subject in the streetlight is thus singular and subjective. So why do we feel so familiar with it, so bored? As if in this unique occurrence we were rereading the same four lines on a box of Cheerios. Or we're stuck on the same scene of a daytime movie we've watched a dozen, hundred times, feeling the picayune blues, recoiling from tedium. I'm dating myself."

He smiles, and on the screen there appears an iStock image, still overlayed by watermark, of an adolescent male in a hoodie in a parking lot at night. He slinks along the door of a white Lexus, radiating menace.

"If you've done this job long enough, it happens. There's going to be bore-dom. But depending on the line of etcetera there may be other reactive events, starting with broad strokes—indifference, negativity—and flowing out into sensations that, given a moment of consideration, of feeling, will reveal themselves as emotions. Anger. A very potent and volatile ember of anger, usually in the chest, throat, or face. A generalized sense that some-thing is off, not-right, as the suspect pivots in the streetlight, in your field of perception. What this usually boils down to is fear. The suspect, then, isn't one individual. He or she arises together with the memory of all other suspects, in lived and virtual experience, life-event and fiction, colouring and toning the suspect's material properties, layering atop it, merging with it—as if this particular suspect were so intolerably radiant as to require camouflage. The suspect is unstable, decohering, luminous as a gas giant, and yet your chin's tucked, so to speak, and eyes lowered. You're flipping through a picture book of suspects somewhere in your head. *Law & Order* and *The Wire*. What is this if not a habit? When did it begin? When will it end? I'm not saying this is intention, but if you're just going to let it happen time and again until retirement then, well, you're a co-conspirator."

Some of them are slipping three-rings and notebooks into backpacks, screwing lids on Nalgenes and Gatorades. There's an accusation settling in the air, finding its electric feet, so he charges into the gathering buzz.

"I feel it's like this. The instant I see and hear the suspect, the suspect becomes untenable as a singular phenomenon due to a host of scary reasons, and I consciously ignore that radiance as such out of fear; one thousand other suspects, both monstrous and comforting, arise to take its place. And I'm flooded with competing emotions for how to deal with both the real and imagined. By now I've become aware of myself seeing and hearing the suspect—not just aware but conscious of that awareness. Then I become aware of myself becoming aware of myself seeing and hearing the suspect. Yes? And again: another link on a chain, a weave that stretches into endless repetition. Encountered for micro-divisions of seconds, the real is buried so far beneath deluge that there is no more real, or no real I can confidently point to. If I close my eyes and look again it begins again. Is this your experience? Looping back, creating, then re-creating, then re-creating, etcetera, ad nauseum, the suspect?"

The mood has indeed shifted, he feels.

"This is happening within the suspect, toward you, the constable or the cadet-in-training. Suspects and officers fluttering inside ourselves, encountering flapping mirages, pentimento. Endlessly creating duplicating copies like a thin-leafed dictionary, a bible caught in a gale. Some part of the real remains, though, like a burnt afterimage, a nuclear shadow or a determined tether of radiance. So the suspect creates me, too, through its living dispensations. How you appear alongside your own list of etcetera is caused by a mere fraction of your actual bearing or intention; the suspect has their experiences, their home movies and stories, to replace your own luminosity, your vivid three dimensions. Let's just say it: I cannot form a perception of, nor hold in conscious awareness, a suspect that does not immediately and equally hold me, and so we dance each other across the sidewalk, the broken asphalt, the burnt-out traffic lights, clutching tightly our indifference and resentment, as tight as a pair of handcuffs. Snugly incarcerated."

He feels panic in the digression, too long veering off the point, so determines to speak rapidly, to bring things to climax.

"But suppose now in this putative scenario there's no suspect at all. Take it a step further. There's no brick wall behind the suspect, no generic Lexus sedan, no distant Walmart parking lot, no tents and collapsible shelters, no susurrating traffic or far-flung tocsins. Not even the moderate May air smelling of forsythia and crabapple, compost and mild petrichor—nothing. What I'm evoking is lacunae. Work with me—you can hold a void here, in imagination, resting in those hard polypropylene seats—but by deductions there's no me in this hypothetical tableau. The me described, the subjective first-person I've been using heretofore, would vanish. And not like the blurry afterimage of the suspect I imagine in the psychedelic neon of my closed eyes. More deeply absent—all the way gone. I am aware so long as there is something to be aware of. Even a sable, silent field is something to be aware of. It would reveal its richness to you over millennia, for example, if you were forced inside it, in some kind of prison sentence. So if we delete the suspect and his entire milieu then we cannot exist either. We become inmates together, to continue the penal metaphor, but even that fails to strike at the codependence I'm trying to help you visualize. S, u, s, p, e, c, t and o, f, f, i, c, e, r: each letter a fractal of etcetera, the phonetic, the acoustic wave, the ubiquitous, shallow fear."

There's murmuring, and laughter, and bags zipped and binders snapped— sounds meant as resistance, and an indication that the minute hand is reaching twelve on the wall clock. It's imminently time to go.

"Do you get outside the city, hit the trails? Do any camping? We're trying to silence an echo while hollering down a mountain stream: the root was there in the voice. And you can't find the answer to this predicament by scanning the night for echoes—especially when your mouth is in fact clamped shut, either by inexperience or fear of legislature or policy. Officers and suspects are on the same stretch of provincial concrete. Badge numbers and criminal records alike come from one source in the floral May evening, shape-shifting principles, exchanging foundations, procreating right, wrong, innocence, and guilt."

They're rising now, speaking over him; the first few bodies stream from the room, pulled through the open door like clods or dross in water through a drain. He doesn't raise his voice.

"So no suspects exist—even amid all our real and imagined hideouts and seedy dens, our commercial havens of embezzlement and fraud—without the invention of officers. A suspect is a play of light, space, heat, liquid and earth, wind and thought, organs and neurons, revving up a habitual machine coiled so tightly in process and code that it runs without oversight. Now, somewhere, there's a suspect making an officer as we speak—legs splayed, palms and forehead kissing a brick wall, whimpering under a sky of teal and firelight spatter. Officer and suspect interlace like gears in one judicial machine; it's not coiled in the officer, or not merely. It represents a totality: a wholeness of springs, pulleys, switches, and guts. But I think the original question was about choice, wasn't it? Meaning, is your shirt sleeve unavoidably caught in the mechanism? Do you slide without protest into the filleting cuspids of the shredder, get swept along into the clockwork of the crushing pistons? If you do, your Glock 17's going to get unstrapped; you're certainly going to feel a snap, and four clean holes will appear on the chest, and not even the reverberations will register with you. In a breath, the clean-up team will be shaking sand onto the road to absorb pools of red. That's why there's boot camp and basic training, why cadets think like soldiers; it's a commitment not to think, but act, without the burden of self-checks—to lift the firearm as an automatic reflex without any real determination to kill. But choice—that's the question. Can you take a backward step instead? Is it even possible, or are we wearing probation anklets? I'm saying that if it's possible, it's crucial: taking a backward step from the jaws. Could we notice what's behind the mechanism's reflex? If everything you are depends on the suspect, then what's there without one—what's the thing that's aware of what's arising? Who exactly is dragging around these black uniforms and body armour, these standard-issue tools?"

The last of them are gone. Once clouded by bodies, exhalations, hormones, now the details of the room re-emerge. The Aegean murk, the beam of the projector, the connected laptop's heated whirr filling the new quiet, the curving desks and haunted monitors. His voice almost breaks.

"If suspects create officers—if we're cuffed to one another—then we're cuffed to every little thing. There's nothing special about suspects, nothing special about officers. So it's one thing, whatever it is. It makes and reflects suspects and officers. It reflects your shaved face in the mirror, your wrist moving a pen across paper. It reflects the unchanging face of the moon, which never turns, within the dent of a Lexus. And if it's all one thing, it's one piece of jewellery. Some would call it a pearl. We can call it one polished badge, a silver beaver crouched on a golden crest, in which arises every cadet-in-training, constable, sergeant, detective, inspector, superintendent, deputy, and chief. Every summary, every indictable or hybrid offender, every teddy bear and pacifier, every hero. And if so, we want to take care of ourselves. If so, we want to take great care of this one thing, this flawless badge. Those who do become responsible—are *personally* responsible, and for every little thing, which means every single suspect. They're personally responsible for every mess, mistake, critical error, offence, and conviction. They take personal responsibility for every sentencing, for every probation. They're on the hook. They're accountable. They are personally responsible for every outcome. And that goes for every gunshot, every chokehold, every suspect that is one no longer and now merely part of everything else."

# MOTIVATION

I LIKE TO ask myself, "What's the point?" Do I shore a tax-free savings account and pay my Visa bill on time to accrue good credit or, you know, do I buy that Louis Vuitton duffle bag—the most divine expense and expression of cupidity? Here I am, doing crunches on floors of drifting dog hair, willing grooves and rivulets to deepen in my abdomen to conquer all those numberless Budweisers of my salad days. Showering the sweat and deathly skin from my body. Applying sweet-smelling tinctures. Dwelling on the fact I haven't had a raise in over a year due to bad financial management at work, feeling victimized. No Christmas bonus, frozen salary, layoffs for buddies. Scanning jobs on LinkedIn and Rogers, Goodwork and Indeed. Imagining the cover letter contortions, the new lies I'll cobble, the bottom rungs on ladders scratching exposed ceilings near Spadina and Queen. The purple-haired boy who stares too long on the streetcar, who glances away then back again—he's suddenly my husband, his problems my problems, his scratchy limbs impossible to disentangle from as he mumbles cartoon nonsense in sleep, our private jokes and silly names (I call him "pizza slice," he calls me "Sully"!) rubbed daily like mala beads to ward off the question. My most precious one. Lying in bed for another five minutes dwelling on ruin and abuse or getting up and getting on with it. Bullet journaling. Konmari-ing my wardrobe. An absurd erection, a fantasy about a person who kissed me a decade ago, who said I should find her in Berlin (or was it Los Angeles?) and that we should cry while snow falls in quiet desolation UpOn AlL tHe LiViNg aNd ThE DeAd. Getting up in the night for a piss and knowing with certainty there's very little time left, that dreaming brings you wherever your karma decides, but with enough effort you might control your mind always, in every state, even in deepest night. It was Berlin.

But what's the point? I like to ask myself this, anyway. Such immense effort, you think, rolling over onto new pillow drool, refusing to awaken, when all you have to lose is sleep. The effort to improve yourself, endlessly, but what's it matter if it's only your own suffering you'll ever feel? Buying a bungalow outside Toronto, commuting in and out in my parents' Ford Focus in solitude or paying my lucky rent here in the city and doing nothing at all. Agreeing to social engagements with friends to rehash the same quests, drinking too much beer as part of the set-up, and the next day's towering headache. This is normally where I'd start to insert the point. Pull up out of the muck of the quotidian and march toward meaning, or aesthetic beauty. But I feel stuck now, as if dreaming, as if asking out of instinct, believing so hard that the funhouse I've entered or the winding highway I've found myself on is really real. Like, it's real, dude. I can say that very little of what I do has a point to it, a *telos* and *logos*. And everything I use is determined first by its function, and this function quietly saps the wonder from my life. A million discs of sunlight pixelating, fusillading, on an ancient maple in the alley, but it's merely a spot of shade on my bored meander; a coffee mug's smooth and hilarious shape created almost entirely by mind, mug of impossible form and yet no form, but it's mainly about moving caffeine into my greedy little mouth. I say I like to ask myself, "What's the point?" but the answers overwhelm and lead back into bottomless shame. By asking myself, "What's the point?" am I really asking, "What's my motivation?" As if I were an actor, someone like Marlon Brando or Val Kilmer, someone with chops.

After the unbearable movie *Suicide Squad* came out there were these click-bait listicle things, these ads. They were all over the internet, and they all showed pictures of Jared Leto dressed up like a clown in a white tuxedo with a variation of the same caption: "You won't believe how far Jared Leto went when playing the Joker," or "These actors went to insane lengths to maintain their roles." I didn't click on any of these advertisements but imagined someone doing so on some wasted, unemployed afternoon in dazzling winter twilight, feeling cheated, and a sadness opened in me. "What's my motivation?" Literally, what motivates me to do what I'm doing right this instant? Is it fame and renown or pleasure and acquisition? It certainly isn't infamy, pain, poverty, and loss. My body needs no motivation to wake up; so long as I do what feels nominally good—dribble it some water, give it a bite of food, and sleep—I will continue, with or without motivation. Even as things break down and I begin to smell like what I am: a tubular worm, a bag of shit. Or I can do the minimal things required and subsist, become like a calico who barely moves, who sleeps in the same armchair in shafts of heavenly sunlight all day because, as my childhood Kerouac said, "it knows there is nothing to do." Here I'm cowed into moving the dishes from the drying rack back into their strict accommodations. I reply to emails from work and clear tickets in their queue. I acknowledge texts from the Joker, someone fanatically committed to their worldview, talk about meeting to discuss chaos and sublimity, incel culture and Joaquin Phoenix, the moon's zoom to the earth. Go back to drifting asleep beneath an ocean of piss. Even this thingy here, this operation, this transmission into your eyes, this marring of a page, deserves more from me, but I struggle to name it. Why put insufficient words to a limitless, confused ache unless you have your motivations cold as math? Why share this with another person unless you've got your lines down pat? Is Poetry the God of Lust, burning at the centre of the wheel? Is it the job of any actor to make you forget she's pretending?

So we've failed, but we've arrived somewhere as well. What I suppose this is for, and why this machine has been screwed together, after all this half-cooked jawing and half-formed sludge, has been to love you in a most genuine way, purple-haired boy and lost girl in Berlin, and Jared Leto and Jack Kerouac, and Pooh Bear, too. And you: to give love to you, without preference or awareness of your faults, and in fact to love you for them, and as much as I could love anyone, like my mother and my father, my only daughter. And to make you know in some way deeper than words that your pain exists inside me, too, and we can croak over it together—but to get there we have to move in a funny, crabwise way so that we don't feel too awkward, or uncomfortable. For you and I need to be handled very delicately, like the big monologue in your movie, or a seed from an extinct tree, or a spiderling or pup in a hanging basket, the last egg of the Dodo, or the world's most precious jewel that, if polished and protected and set on a pillow of purple velvet, might one day wipe away the pain and sorrow of all the poor suffering creatures in the world, so long as it had the right motivation.

III

# THE GARBAGE AND OIL THREAD

*In tribute to Eihei Dōgen zenji's "Sansuikyō" (1240 CE)*

I

THE GREAT PACIFIC Garbage Patch, much like the Deepwater Horizon oil spill, has been around since before the Big Bang. They're both still vibing today, so they can't overshoot any tipping points or timelines. Neither pretend to be anything but what they are. Neither sport a resumé, a persona or god-tier avatar, so they're just like you and me when we don't fill out a bio. In fact, they're perfect mentors; they exhaust themselves teaching. You can pick their grimy brains for free, and once schooled, make lateral and horizontal moves, enjoying trade winds two thousand feet above the sea.

2

A heap of high-density polyethylene walks around nonstop; a *Top Gun: Maverick* Barbie Doll lays an egg for a black-footed albatross.

Because there's no stain on the Great Pacific Garbage Patch, it's at peace with itself, chilling. It came preloaded with the awesome quality of being the Great Pacific Garbage Patch. It's never not getting premium circadian rest, and it's never not getting in its ten thousand steps, in absolute productivity beast-mode, gyring faster than a hurricane roiling to the coast. It may not look similar to the way you or I walk, manipulating our legs over the mezzanines, limping from one Telus kiosk to another, but that's exactly how the Great Pacific Garbage Patch is walking. And that's why it's here forever.

If you arose moment by moment within the Great Pacific Garbage Patch, like a sakura flower making the whole world turn to spring on a Hello Kitty nurdle, you might not catch the impressive velocity—but still, you'd be in the real world, with no way in and no way out. Thus, you can imagine how many folks never give a passing eye to the Great Pacific Garbage Patch, and never know that the way it walks is in fact exactly how they walk. This means they likely don't even know themselves. Sad.

If the Great Pacific Garbage Patch isn't aware, then we aren't aware; if we're aware, then the Great Pacific Garbage Patch is aware—but that's not quite right either. Getting this isn't about cramming for your GRE or LSAT. You can't be correct on *Jeopardy* even in the form of a question, can't turn to metric or imperial, to Planck, Stoney, or Hartree units. But what you can do is go forward with ten thousand hands. What you *can* do is turn back, examine those quads of bone and meat, and flip the switch inside your head. You can do both, even at the same time, and won't fuck up either way. Just know that if you stop walking, or the Great Pacific Garbage Patch stops walking, then this conversation isn't happening.

So what's the Great Pacific Garbage Patch? Walking? A plastic bucket? A sakura bud? The sum of its nurdles? We at Little Mind Ltd. circle back on emails when there's a dearth of replies. The Great Pacific Garbage Patch circles back on itself, earning a doctorate in self-knowledge, and all thanks to our present consideration. And speaking of doctorates: I know a narcissist, a communist, a pulmonologist, a senior video-game designer, and a search engine optimization specialist, and they all have the same disconsolate thought: that the Great Pacific Garbage Patch can't flow and can't walk. They don't know that the Great Pacific Garbage Patch is the vital artery of their snoozing life.

Sure, my bank manager, dental hygienist, and academic adviser pals tell me, "Sir, the Great Pacific Garbage Patch is actually a pile of water bottles, gas canisters, dragnets, gum wrappers, Bic lighters, fishhooks, asthma inhalers, chum buckets, cigarette packets, and bike sprockets," but that's not a complete picture. My plumber, Hegelian influencer, and OnlyFans friends might say instead, "the petroleum vortex is incandescent in the sunlight, a vision of sublime rapture," but who wants to live there? Even if, blissed out on hot yoga and CBD oil, you make the Great Pacific Garbage Patch a seven-day retreat—or even the embodiment of all that's lowercase holy—you're still staring through a banned plastic straw. It's enough to say, simply, that the Great Pacific Garbage Patch walks, because otherwise there's going to be you and it, and it and you, and every concept you cook up is designed to make the Patch stay still.

3

On a moonless night, you can't tell chunks of the Great Pacific Garbage Patch apart; when the "sun's sublime rapture" hits, the Patch breaks into thread and microplastic, filth and integrity. Now pause for a brief story: on one level, my dental hygienist friend decides to have a baby. She monitors ovulation, kicks the booze and cigs, takes supplements, and then gets a blue line on her pregnancy stick. *Boom*—she's a mom; her child is Mia or Hunter. All of this happens in the dreary noonday sun. But on another level, when a bottle of Diet Sprite, made of high-density polyethylene, lays an egg for *Phoebastria nigripes*, it's totally dark, and cause and effect converge. Mia and Hunter baby their mother. Every instance is its own frozen LCD screen. Every moment, you lay an egg from which the Great Pacific Garbage Patch hatches and gets redeemed by your consideration. Every present moment, the Great Pacific Garbage Patch is A/B testing new polymers in your veins, becoming and considering you.

4

The Great Pacific Garbage Patch flows on water and walks on land. At night, there's no Pacific Ocean, no "Greatness" to the Patch, and nothing keeping garbage separate from "store-bought with original packaging intact." It's one thing and it's billions, trillions of things. It appears as a saint, a TED Talk, and a personal mentor, whom you can use to verify a truth from before the Big Bang, past all our Davos-drawn tipping points, dumping us into "worst case scenarios" for me, for you, sakura buds and the ill-fated black-footed albatross.

5

I think you'd agree that even among so-called smart people—MFA graduates, foreign correspondents, former *Gawker* reporters—there's a ton who don't know anything about garbage piles or oil spills or the value of their own consideration of them. To take the case of poetry, some MFA grads think saying, "The Great Pacific Garbage Patch walks nonstop" is a kind of mystical metaphor, not meant to be understood rationally ("it's meant to be read and appreciated on its own terms, differently, without recourse to reason"). People who say this are infants and dimmer than puppies. They're worse than that clichéd fifty-nine-year-old in Whitehorse who's writing a cringey romance novel in secret and they're worse than your average dietician, mechanic, or Pita Pit wrapper who never reads poetry, period. Searing your brain with spare, inscrutable lines of verse until you cannot think, cannot see oceanic destruction or your responsibility for it, is not our present objective. You have to see a connection between having a wild, selfish latte-brain and the genuine possibility of poetry, all without pretending you don't in fact bloom in the middle of the Great Pacific Garbage Patch, causing another Anthropocene extinction.

6

Somewhere out in the vast Pacific Ocean, the real moon makes a bone-white road on a black lane of marrow, and it points to a real heap of garbage. Somewhere in the Gulf of Mexico, the Deepwater Horizon oil spill squirts a soapy ribbon of rust, squash, marmalade, and sandstone the size of Oklahoma, and it snakes to the stiff, pewter corpse of a dolphin crusting on a stony beach, smiling to heaven. Garbage and oil are beyond abstraction. Oil is oil in the midst of the Great Pacific Garbage Patch, and the Great Pacific Garbage Patch is every pile of refuse everywhere, in every landfill and KFC, even scoring the moon like a spy balloon above our heads, or like a simile of marrow and bone. It is always splashing and bobbing freely, as if TikTok dancing in a pool of oil.

7

You can walk on oil once it reaches a certain hypothetical temperature, but one degree lower and you'll sink right through—down into its milky innards. You can deep-fry fowl with a tank and stainless-steel basket, and you can refresh a plastic Wendy's salad with a splash of olives, pressed. You can coat an adorable marine mammal with whiskers and paws, or wrap a black chador of crude around an elegant mallard's beak, concealing its sex. Oil is precious upon Aaron's head, his curly beard, dripping thickly upon his robes. It's the oil of love, sweeter than wine, near the tents of Kedar; it oozes from fat squeezed from the burnt offering of Karystos goats. Silky soft, it's I Can't Believe It's Not Butter, and it anoints the pistons and cylinders of a colonial F-35. And quite literally there is no oil, and no Deepwater Horizon: it is paraffin, olefin, naphthene; it's alkanes, cycloalkanes, and aromatic hydrocarbons. Quite literally, there are no hydrocarbons. Because it shuns an essence, no one can break or smash, cut, cancel, or write a think piece on the Deepwater Horizon oil spill. And yet here we are, cleaning it up dutifully—passing bills, levying fines, reading BP as apocalypse, moisturizing our lips with peppermint.

A tiny dude on a two-man skiff in the Gulf, gazing at the sinuous crude, the infernal plume, speaking Spanish on a VHF, is actually the Deepwater Horizon oil spill looking at itself, speaking Deepwater Horizon oil spill. It becomes the Deepwater Horizon oil spill through this tiny dude's tiny, wearisome eyes, which have seen a lot of feelings. Now, to be practical: show me a tiny dude on a two-man skiff in the Gulf who doesn't see the oil as tragic, or as elegy, or as fuel for a lamp, or as the name poured out most redolently in the bedchambers of the King. Show me a guy who sees oil as oil, just *oil*, and not a feature of his own tornadic bipolar disorder. Show me a tiny dude on a boat in the Gulf speaking "tiny dude on a boat in the Gulf."

8

From high above, the Deepwater Horizon oil spill is a skein of suds in some alien's sink, or a garland of ruby, citrine, topaz, and garnet. From higher still, it's a fleck or speck on our blue marble, then nothing at all. The oil's the Milky Way to its microbial inhabitants—a corporate palace, a backdrop of suffering, so familiar in its unremarkableness. We see the oil as a killer, *The Blob*; it's death on Pensacola Beach; a way the white croaker tastes kinda weird and a pelican dooms its chicks. A miracle of combustion, it's why Chad remortgaged his bungalow for a new Dodge Durango. It's also *casus belli* to scramble the F-117 Nighthawks, which liberate an ancient city two thousand pounds per drop. For some, oil's a raging flame, a pillar of smoke, turning day to night in the deserts of Kuwait. Yet, in every case, oil appears. It manifests. It sits exactly as and where it is—say a slick, oozing for 155,000 square kilometres—and from that precise position does not move an inch.

Every misdeed engenders a judgment. Every judgment is cooked up by a user, and with no apparent release. So ask yourself: is the Deepwater Horizon oil spill one thing, merely seen from different sides—grey alien, microbial, Spanish Mackerel, or Republican? Or are there only billions of angles, and each one incomplete? Is oil *oil* before we burn, clean, extract, or murder for it? Or does killing for oil make it oil to begin with?

There's no other Deepwater Horizon drilling platform. No other rig sits in repose on the Macondo Prospect. And yet, it walks—the Deepwater Horizon oil spill is free of the Macondo Prospect. Sitting on the Macondo

Prospect in the Northeastern Gulf of Mexico lets all that dirty oil go. The oil's always safe and snug in its cement well. It's always free to visit South America. Like Mia and Hunter—babies forever, yet free of their nappies, and free to baby their mother.

That way the Deepwater Horizon oil spill demonstrates an unspeakable wonder, and right on our screens. Even my dental hygienist friend, despite being a dental hygienist, is liberated from being a dental hygienist, defying latte-brain sense. Her life liberates itself from her life, which means she's also free to be anything, including a mother, or dead. Or the Deepwater Horizon oil spill.

9

When I say "oil," you see varying weights and colours, organic and mineral versions of some kind of gloop. But essentially, you see a liquid of medium viscosity that obeys the laws of physics—dribbling from high places to low, settling in crevices, seeping down canisters, spilling out into slicks. You see a flow. But oil is also oil when it evaporates into gas, or boils into vapour; oil is the smoke from a burn, or crud baked in August. Oil forms carbon dioxide and water. Eventually, oil disappears, but it also seeps through every stone, apron, or bladder, beyond what we can imagine: into the sea, or into a lawnmower engine; onto your spaghetti or across the horizon; out of earth's upper mantle and back into fire. It's in anesthesia and ghazals and dreams, and on a Chrome internet browser. It's in the mind of the intern and that of the perfect mentor. Even people with PornHub accounts get this—they just can't articulate it. The average viewer of *Fox & Friends* knows more about oil than the great sages of antiquity, so let's not bury secular people in our sprint toward liberation.

Oil does its oily thing without thinking about it and without not thinking about it. It does it on autopilot, in a state of flow, as per Nakamura and Csikszentmihalyi. Yet with all the majesty of what oil can do, do you think knowing or not knowing really matters? Do you think knowing will hone its craft, or not knowing hold it back?

We talk of deep subsurface reservoirs. Of tar pits and stratigraphic traps. Spurts, or gushers. Wells and distillation towers. Pipelines, barrels, pools and slicks, spills and jerry cans. All these containers, named conveniently in the English language, come after oil, and serve only as oil's temporal positions. Oil is the primordial movement. Even in the Gulf of Mexico, it's essence-less flowing—it is not the Deepwater Horizon whatsoever.

Blake writes, in "Auguries of Innocence,"
    To see a World in a Grain of Sand
    And a Heaven in a Wild Flower
    Hold Infinity in the palm of your hand
    And Eternity in an hour

So let's imagine the tiniest drop of oil from the Deepwater Horizon contains a universe more richly appointed than the Mos Eisley cantina on Tatooine, or an antediluvian grammar. The oil isn't trapped in 2010 and neither does it flow on tomorrow, but every moment—from before the Big Bang to the sun's retirement. Each drop is the middle cell of a quadruple-venn diagram, meaning space, present, forever, and whatever dope's there to experience it.

Hence the importance of the perfect mentor, who goes wherever the oil slick floweth, she who can see the Deepwater Horizon oil spill walking around nonstop, and correct our straw-filtered frameworks. We must learn not to capture it, but to see it as that vital artery we spoke of earlier—to see all the ways it walks are exactly how we are walking. If you told some obligate hydrocarbonoclastic bacteria, like *Oleispira* and *Alcanivorax*, that they were microscopic cell envelopes that live within smarter species—or that the oil they live in and eat was a measurable environmental disaster, by the tonne and gallon—they'd never believe you for a second. To them, oil is the total horizon. Likewise, we say the pumpjack points up and the hollow drill goes down. We stand still, while the piston pump nods and the mud pump moves fluid. The sky's above us, the oil below, bacteria inside us, and our feet stand on a rig tethered securely to the ocean's floor. But where's right-side up or upside down if we're rotating 1,670 kilometres per hour and shooting around the sun at 107,826 kilometres per hour? Our dwelling is walking, yet we say we need to get more daily exercise.

Belinda Carlisle said it best when she sang, "Heaven is a place on earth." In the same way, we know that hell's not below us in some *Far Side* cavern; for those suffering, it's the whole fluid universe. A heap of high-density polyethylene walks around non-stop. A *Top Gun: Maverick* Barbie Doll lays an egg for the black-footed albatross.

10

From before the Big Bang to the ungraspable present, perfect mentors have made the Great Pacific Garbage Patch their penthouse, start-up incubator, and corner office. For them, the garbage is more than a state of grind. It's their whole body; there's no inside or outside. We might think we can find these mentors there, inhabiting the Patch, but when we do what they've done, we find they've ghosted us. If we do what they do, we ghost ourselves. We leave behind our resumés and portfolios and become part of the slosh—there's no trace of footprints on hectares of nurdles.

From outside, you can fire up your browser and see a North Pacific subtropical mountain; a mass at the centre of eighty thousand tonnes and a loose, less easily circumscribed enclosure, with a total range of two States of Texas. An image search will yield a junk heap of Evian bottles, Husky waste bags, and myriad McDonald's takeout containers, going nowhere. As with our perfect mentors, being inside the Patch makes it look much different. May our interning phase show us we've never been estranged from it; let us see how it manifests in very mundane ways within us. May we learn from the microbial devourers, the wounded sea turtles, and the grey aliens beyond comprehension. Let's absorb what we can from perfect mentors from beyond the past and present: trust that not only is the Great Pacific Garbage Patch getting perfect rest, but that it never stopped moving.

II

If you don't want to be trapped in a cycle of bad habits, locked into your generalized anxiety disorder, your nihilism and unconscious bias, then don't disrespect the perfect mentors mentioned here. Don't disrespect "The Garbage and Oil Thread," meaning, garbage and oil are always resting and always on the make. This injunction is about banal shit and theoretical physics; it's been tatted onto plastic, concrete slab, and marijuana fields, onto megalopolises and agribusiness monocrops. You should tattoo them on your face like Post Malone, on your inner lip like Kendall Jenner. You should research inner organ tattoos and write these words on your liver, and you should ensure they're inscribed on your wireless network. You should tattoo them on your eyes so what you see is constantly true.

Obviously, the Great Pacific Garbage Patch goes beyond national borders; it's not owned by any president or prime minister. But if you love it and take care of it, then it belongs to you. You belong to it—you enter the Patch and the Patch enters you. You'll feel, too, that the Great Pacific Garbage Patch is simping for you hard. With your consideration, those feedlot bags, hypodermic needles, truck tires, paint cans, funeral ashes, and Ziploc sacs flourish and become inspired.

A president or prime minister crushes on fame, happiness, praise, and gain. It's the same with the whole C-suite and D-suite of courtiers, fawning over ideology. The perfect mentor among the floating particles has no such lust. That's why we all, from interns to great world leaders making seven-plus figures, come to stand on the Great Pacific Garbage Patch; it's where we pray for instruction, taking a knee in yard waste, rocks of bitumen and ribbons of leather, with zero resentment. How else? Even among all their economic calculations, how could the world's richest person alter anything we've thought? We're using thinking to get out of the nastiest cycles of thinking; they're not.

For ages, folks have tried to strike oil, as in major motion pictures like *Boom Town* (1940), *Blowing Wild* (1953), *There Will Be Blood* (2007), *Armageddon* (1998), or even *Deepwater Horizon* (2016), starring Mark Wahlberg as Chief

Electronics Technician Michael Williams, which dramatized the event and its walking. Such folk strike oil. Some strike the rig, some strike themselves, and some get struck by oil. The oil pumps the crew and the oil pumps itself, and our heartbeats. By watching these strong, blue-collared labourers work, mourn, say the Lord's Prayer, speak invariably in accents from Massachusetts, we might realize none of them are striking, no one's getting struck, yet nonetheless we are showered in petroleum. We go to the movies to meet an oil-covered Mark Wahlberg, losing ourselves and meeting ourselves in the darkness of petrocinema.

12

So it goes without saying that the Deepwater Horizon oil spill is not only in the Gulf of Mexico, but there's a Gulf of Mexico—littered with miniature mouth-breathers—within the oil. It's the same with salad dressing, gas turbine engines, gouts of flame, and *Fox & Friends*. Wherever there's miniature mouth-breathers, there's an S-tier of perfect mentors, enjoying equanimity, and a whole host of miserable fucks, dragging their legs from one Telus kiosk to another. Oil is where the dragons of *Dragons' Den* live, unmoving within the flow, yet moving endorsements within the solid gunk. Oil is simply as it is: you cannot bring it to a court of fluid mechanics, demand to measure how it flows or doesn't, or to restrict its buoyancy or surface tension. To do so would be akin to foisting your fledgling business venture upon Arlene Dickinson or Mr. Wonderful, and without evidence of profitability, scalability, and good management—an insult.

There is garbage within retirement savings accounts, and garbage in Lake Simcoe, and garbage behind the sun, and garbage within garbage. We used the phrase, "staring through a banned plastic straw," but we're cutting out metaphors in this last graduate workshop. We're not saying that the Great Pacific Garbage Patch is the Great Pacific Garbage Patch, or the Deepwater Horizon oil spill is the Deepwater Horizon oil spill. We're saying that garbage is garbage and oil is oil. Studied like this, garbage and oil will, as in *The Help* (2011), spontaneously make you smart, make you kind, and make you important.

IV

# THE HELL OF LAUGHTER

TWO TWENTY-FIVE-YEAR-OLD girls flip-flop through languid summer heat toward the public swimming pool in High Park, Toronto. They wear shorts and baggy tees over neon bathing suits. They shoulder towels in mesh bags, heavy with novels, water bottles, and SunnyD. One of them wears a *Wayne's World* trucker hat. They are tan-lined and spotty, enormous sunglasses slipping down noses still greasy from SPF 30. All the subway ads on the way were misspelled or about vibrators, and one girl, Marigold, feels like crying as she drags on her vaporizer. Not because of what her guru told her over Skype, but merely because she feels stupid—tricked for so long by the lovely promises of her graduate degree. She feels like arguing about it now, in a vague way. The other girl, Black-Eyed Susan, is a genuine artist, someone who cannot stop thinking about bodily experiences, has pure motivations to provide verisimilitude to the vividness of suchness. She is a poet. But she has a perverse fixation, Marigold feels, with the imitation of reality, and not with the mechanical ability to make someone laugh and cry with made-up stories. The argument simmers as they reach the chlorinated water. Black-Eyed Susan thinks, *Every time I open my mouth, something new is ruined, so maybe I'll just shut up forever.*

I am writing a novel, in the twenty-seventh year of my life, combating a recurring sense that nothing I can write will make a difference or add to or take away from anything else in the world, and nothing will solve the central hurt of my invented life, a separate self-image among all the weaponry of the universe. And yet I am desperate and determined to be read. I believe wholeheartedly that I can be a novelist, and despite my misgivings about my talents and motivations, I should persevere. I am sweating through tight white T-shirts in my second-floor apartment in a summer of work and beer, headaches, delirium and sex, Burger King, espressos, trees as lurid as giallo films on Roncesvalles Avenue. The streetcars trolley me along College Street to a youth hostel, my temporary workplace, a hole I cannot crawl back inside, where I spend long evenings reading and rewriting my novel. I dreamed of a photograph: me in an expensive peacoat in a half-page column in the *Globe and Mail*, my hair looking really good, standing before bricks and graffiti, and a headline about what it means to live in the world today, in the eternal floating present. My expensive taste in martinis and outfits and lists of things "in" and "out," printed in little art-store pamphlets. A novel is the precise accessory, a charm in a wallet full of my parents' money. I have imagined a series of events, a rhythm of sound, a mirror ball of faces, a thematic configuration. Timelines, flashbacks, abstractions, arousals. But the thing that flies up is a rhyming couplet, annoyingly: me and my best friend seemed so different, but now that she's dead, I am the same person. The laundry basket was something we owned together. White plastic from China, sitting mutely in a column of dust.

Meanwhile, another girl is riding a bus, and her name is Spencer, like me, because girls can be named Spencer now in the 2010s (like in *Pretty Little Liars* or like the real-life daughter of *Frasier* star, Kelsey Grammer). Spencer lowers her eyes, ashamed, as she watches a man carrying an antique stereo in Bloorcourt. Pop lyrics rise like thousands of sparrows, taking the air as one monster, thrilling Spencer's spinal column, saluting the tiny hairs of her lower back. She catches the passing whiff of beach sand and deep fryers, seagulls and freedom, awakening a memory of an adventure during a heat wave in 2001, back when she strode through heaps of garbage and lilies, feeling like a willing sacrifice to something old. She lowers her eyes, ashamed, because most of those hopes have withered. Most of her is gone. She glances down to a novel, as if medicinal, sitting in her lap; she swivels an iPhone in her digits; she reads sixteen ads lining the bus, misspelled and sexual, and the bus shouldn't even be running, but the subway is down, and through the drone of a baby's dental yowl she vibrates over potholes to visit an older man who's preparing her will. She's hot in her socks. She wants to go home, get drunk, and work on her art. A pathetic summer storm roils the horizon and rages through Microsoft. The lady beside her has a mouth stained with merlot, smelling like tomorrow's hangover, and she leans close to Spencer and says, with the voice of a black widow, "Don't trust anybody."

I pause my work, leaning out the window of my rental unit, shared with men who don't shower, who sleep until two o'clock, who leave mugs of coffee in their rooms to go sticky and leave the sinks full of curly hair. I tap a pen against my teeth and wonder: what comes after all this ragged weeping? What comes after the heart-attack bedsheets? What comes after the monstrous summer storm? In my novel, called *The Hell of Laughter*, all the actors roar with this summer fire. Some go unrequited; some are recently divorced. Some dribble tears over revolvers stuck in their mouths, or jump from gothic spires after stock-market plunges, investment errors. Some toil under the delusion that with just a bit more effort, the precise tweaks, they can suffer less and enjoy prolonged summer holidays of pleasure. Some, like Spencer, simply press their foreheads against bus windows, churning spit-flavoured gum in sore cheeks. They finger their novels with peeling award stickers and timely, political guts, telling them how to properly direct their remorse. Back home, in her art, in her own novel, Spencer wants to make them suffer, these phantoms, so that people will get a taste of her custom-fitted anguish, the fresh shock of her disappointments; so they'll share with her the cup of sorrow she bought from Second Cup, where she used to work, wearing the apron, until she fell apart. I'm writing a novel, in this twenty-seventh summer, grad school long behind me, teaching a new kind of hell, and I wonder: what is the cultural value of style? How about mischief? Is it good, collectively, being tickled? Why are incisive critiques better than the ordinary workings of the body and mind, experiencing, experiences, lucidity of an organ in full working order? Why might it be useful to swing the arm back in a broad gesture, as if sweeping dishes from a table, and sum it all up into a pithy comment? I read this book and knew, immediately, it was the book of the year, so to be wry and cagey is to be excellent? To do with your body what your body was born to do, like sweat and chew and have sex, is to be wonderful, but to become ill, to grow ugly or aged, is not so interesting? Of course, it is interesting to mourn, to elicit pity, but not to be undesirable yourself. Is this correct? Is it good to be drunk, breezy, buzzing with name-brand liquor, French 75s and gimlets of Glenfiddich? Everyone wants to be attractive in some scintillating way but also apart from it all: a bit better, less fickle, with a secret sentimentality reserved for intimates, such as readers, your very best pals in the world, who might exhibit a shortlist of admirable, bitchy quirks. Reader, intimacy is not-knowing but it is also perception of the illusory gap. Why is it good to know what it's like to be a certain age, living somewhere particular, like Lyon, London, or Toronto, in a very certain year: 2008, 2011, 2017? The Harlem Renaissance, or the 100 Years War? The Black Plague? Why preserve for others an experience of longing, and pleasure, and youthful joie de vivre? Or that we have plainly different genitals, and precise body chemistries and hormonal compositions? Different obsessions and fixations, things we find attractive and things we've decided are attractive, things we loathe, and all the confusions that ensue from encountering one another: how we do not precisely fit? Grand comedy? Because it is hot outside, in the middle of summer, and we are drunk somewhere in a rented room talking so much we will wake up with ringing ears? I cannot answer these questions today; they support my sense that nothing I write will lift the rock on my head, but still, I wish to be read. I shower in the dank, tie-dye-stained tub, and say goodbye to the sleeping housemates, put on a clean new T-shirt, and board the creaking streetcar to the hostel, where I pretend to work.

I'm writing a novel under the assumption that when it's read, and if it's moving enough, and it makes my readers cry and rage, and invest in the tragedies and comedies of my characters—soulful Black-Eyed Susan, darling Marigold, suffering Spencer, and this novelist, Spencer Gordon— and heave little sighs of recognition, loving the entangled forward-moving and backwards-moving madness of the thing, careful and clever as a watch, that I will rise toward a constellation of stars that, from telescopic angles on earth, detail the great masters of history in equipoise and hastilude. And I will cherish their company, those forbidden and cancelled and those still worshipped, for an eternity of fellow-feeling and praise. I'm writing a novel under the assumption that others will see in me a sensitivity and perception that marks me as distinct from other people trudging along the anterooms and foyers of Lethe and thus will forgive me my trespasses. I'm writing a novel to remember surprising my sweetheart with a disposable camera and how she wheezed and laughed, her eyes sickles over the newspaper; to close the original wound I suffered as a child, beaten in the bathroom by my mother's thundering open palms, or whipped by Daddy in a cloud of talcum on the green carpet; to show the world I am not defenceless, hurt, terrified, humiliated, incompetent, vulgar, odious, cruel, and poor, and I can live a substitute life without those troubles, as a novelist. Here, in this coffee shop, in a white T-shirt, avoiding more work, remembering the Yoda nightlight that said, in a toddler's pout, "disappear they will, all that you cherish and love." Oh, nobody knows my sorrows as I wander this lonely city, possessed of an aged Parisian spirit, syphilitic, charged with obscenity, unwell, swimming with hate and woeful schmaltz. I think of my book in the Service Ontario centre and feel absurd—my teeth and hair coming loose, my friends buried in burlap, makeup around my eyes that makes me look beaten, bruised. The garden of earthly delights swarming in spring with boys in Prada dresses, and a chatty critic in a white-walled gallery with wine-stained gums summing up all I've done by means of denial, what's not on the page, his voice like a black widow, whispering. What I didn't do, didn't even attempt to do. The flowers are dead on the table. Do you see them? The flowers have been dead, the dry petals dropped, the stems rotted, and yet we skim past the dead because the plot is elsewhere—I have eyes, don't I? Tell me something exciting. Make something happen. Make a beginning and an ending that makes me laugh and delight and rage and, yes, if you want me to be drunk, malicious spirit, I will become that way, always drunk, even as you wish me nothing but ill, even as we ascend to starlight, to make our twin constellations among all the laughing devas, luxurious and immaterial, in the four heavens, for a billion years, we few who write novels.

# JOY IS ALWAYS WITH YOU

JOY IS ALWAYS with you! It is always July 1, 10:15 p.m., in Bloor West Village, and you're riding a stream of fifty-eight boys flowing out from *Infinity War*, smelling of Coke and popcorn. It's always 1996, your lips meeting a can of 7 Up in the Pineland Public School forest jewelled with dew with your best friends Dave and Brent. It's always the Mapleview Mall on a Sunday, square skylights of blue and cotton-tailed contrails above, CD racks clacking with electronica in Sunrise Music, where Chris Helmers worked while still in high school. It's always *Little Women* and a cable-knit sweater, great heaving sobs that puff the cheeks but purge the chest. A jolly grey cocker spaniel, caught in love, a mourning dove in your handbag. Joy is always with you: the dance of powdery, starlit snow from the Royal Bank windowsill, the groan of eight hundred elm trees in the Orono Crown Lands sounding in unison like a rutting moose while your dog, Fred, stands with his silken ears at radio attention, and the ragged air rakes your lungs pink. Circumstances are always neutral. The young white carbuncular man living in the rundown Royale Estates sipping a

Red Bull at 2:01 p.m. on a Friday, out of work, trudging toward you in the salt-strewn snow in a knock-off Canada Goose. And his face means anything you want it to: my sweet baby, a threat, a comrade-in-arms. Joy is always with you. The pre-dawn squeaking of rodents in the walls, the rugged Clarington snowplows, the soot-frizzed neighbour with OCD who shovels herself hot at midnight, funnelling the white heaps from her backyard into the barking traffic of night—oh, Venus! Oh, meteors and Roddy Ricch, the squeak-squawk of "The Box," the clapback of Twitter. Dry hands and sore ankles, suspicious eye leak, always the midafternoon glow of October in Ottawa and you, a student in 2007, wearing sunglasses that made the ByWard Market honey brown, Blue Rodeo practicing "Five Days in May" for their surprise set, when you couldn't be lonelier—the leather jacket torn to pieces, the mix CDs destroyed, the frail copy of *King Richard III* you read for "Jacobian Shakespeare" a lump in your flared denim. Nothing is just what it is; there are no Terms and Agreements. It is just this thing, this, oh, thisness, thiscosity, lump. It is always your Cookie Monster pull-string doll that sounded like a demon. It is always your dad dressed as Conky the robot printing off the secret word at your *Pee-wee's Playhouse*–themed birthday party, and your mother's O.G. lasagna and Caesar salad after you ran away in a rage with a bag of jogging pants and toys, and were rescued! This circle is infinite—it includes all things that are and could possibly be, with nothing outside and all in, as your mind now covers the entire universe at the snap of Thanos's Infinity Gauntlet—yes—*snap*—and the boys are home and tired and a mess of wonder and salty dread. Dummy, nothing is what it is unless you want it to be: joy behind your eyes and lips, behind your unspeakably sexy form, behind your great peal of relief.

# THE HORRIBLE INCLEMENCY OF LIFE

### After *Blue Nights* (2011) by Joan Didion

THE POETS WERE wed beneath the blue glass of the evangelists. A clear day, hushed in the chancel of the Church of the Holy Trinity. The bride wore a tulle veil and bore Dendrobium blooms; he gave Bogart in a vintage ivory dinner jacket, flashed talismans from Golden Iron Tattoo. There were llamas present; they spit at a bridesmaid she'd met at Branksome Hall. The cake, a Bobbette & Belle, was matcha, as was the champagne. We met staff from *Maclean's* and *Chatelaine*, the owners of Type, and a compliance manager from Brazzers, for whom she once wrote copy. We listened to "Jesu, Joy of Man's Desiring" on a Casavant, and later, "Still D.R.E." on a Steinway B. The Ubers and Lyfts lined James and Albert, then swam us to the infinity pool at Bisha. We sensed dianella, African lilies, an edible dahlia, and snowstorms of sweet alyssum. I rounded a corner and there, frozen on a landing, was a capybara, who seemed to sleep standing up. *I refuse to inflict punishments on characters in my work*, she told me. *But I'll give no rewards, either.*

Annie Murphy stood panting on the ski slopes of Mont Grand-Fonds. Bruce Greenwood, Sandra Oh. Dining with us at L'Orchidée that winter in Point-au-Pic in Le Manoir Richelieu. August with Ben and Jessica Mulroney's daughter, Isabel Veronica, who preferred the name Ivy. The velvet sand on the Lake of Bays and Shay Mitchell's blazing dock. Girls from Havergal and St. Clement's; Atom Egoyan's homely protégé; pipevine swallowtails at the ceremony. Sarah Polley, Cobie Smulders, Molly Parker, and Xavier Dolan's *Matthias & Maxime*. Brampton's most famous poet sang, "We All Try" by Frank Ocean, ruby earrings catching light, as we released pearl-coloured balloons and watched them bob over Old Toronto toward the Garden District, Cabbagetown. There was a pearl-coloured Yorkipoo snapping at the hornets drawn to the frosting. He'd be writer-in-residence at Simon Fraser in four days, so the poets moved to a dreamy space over English Bay. *We're going to read works that never mention the words class, race, climate, war, and poverty*, he said, *but imply them, atmospherically.*

An open-top Tesla Roadster. The Wychwood and St. Lawrence markets. A boiled wool blanket from Hoi Bo she wore to TIFA, promoting the release of *Do I Do What I Want?* Then New Year's in Türkiye. Windsor sack-back chairs around a farmhouse table at the beach house in New Brunswick, strewn with postcards from Marrakech. Paul Sarossy, the cinematographer; Truefitt & Hill hand soaps he ordered in bulk. Matching raincoats from Everlane, she in her Ferragamo angora, he in Rudraksha seed necklaces, both with rosaries from Uganda. He bought her a challis from Bohème Vintage in Mile End after a panel at Église unie Saint-James as part of Metropolis Bleu. Something about the phrase, from Didion's *Blue Nights*, "Holly's Harp chiffon and lettuce edges and sizes zero and two" wouldn't leave her. It was about mothers and daughters and about clothing and arrangements, costumes and legacy. They made a sitting room. Jericho Beach and crystal glasses in the rain. Lilly Pulitzer worn, ironically, over Coal Harbour, on the windy way to Bowen Island on Tom Power's boat. Elliot Page, Simu Liu, and Allison Hsu; the Paradox Hotel, in the Karma Lounge, fingering the palm fronds. Lunch at Five Sails, where a table was once saved for a fixer for Bindy Johal. Nearby, wrapped tightly in a cashmere stole, a famous Canadian novelist quarrelled bitterly over dinner with her less famous novelist husband. Nadia Litz, Scott Speedman, *Crimes of the Future*. She told me *glamour was part of the spell; that avoiding appearance, especially clothing, was not authenticity but a pose.*

Michael Kors heels at the National Magazine Awards gala. At Garb, a vintage, dove-grey Donald Brooks bought for *Toronto Life*'s Most Influential. A Versace parasol, found at a bargain. He decided to wear only collarless shirts going forward, hanging steamed on thirty wooden hangers: cotton linen in the summer, cotton and flax in the cold. St. James Catholic Church in Summerfield, Prince Edward Island. Stephen Moyer, Anna Paquin's Academy Award for *The Piano*, faience dinner plates, and an antique rattan bassinet. A Karen Millen tweed pencil dress you'd swear was real Chanel and a Hermès bracelet, visible in candid headshots taken by a Torontonian who'd done most of her work for the *New York Times*. *Wearing the Hermès was a way to stoke ambition, longing, in others*, she said. *And to disturb a certain caste of male writer.*

Dion Phaneuf's estate near New London. Elisha Cuthbert, wearing Chanel in textured, icy-blue tweed; a black Toyota Century imported from Japan. A popover dress from 1943. The CEO of Canada's largest publishing house, the Canadian recipient of the world's largest writing prize, a psychologist and memoirist worth over $1.5 billion, and *Crepuscular* from the National Ballet of Canada. He was typing for PEN and she for *Brick*, part-time, and as a mentor with TMU. Bylines in *Elle Canada*, *Fashion*, *Hazlitt*, and a publication dedicated to various pleasures: olfactory, tactile, gustatory. The Drake and the Gladstone and the Broadview in Toronto, the Arc in Ottawa, Le Soleil and L'Hermitage in Vancouver, the Four Seasons in Montreal and W when they couldn't expense the stay. Muir in Halifax, Le Germain in Calgary, the Hyatt House and Mere in Winnipeg. It was at Le Château Frontenac, at Champlain Restaurant, that she read Mary Oliver and Dionne Brand for the first time. She had a sixteen-city book tour: Halifax, Fredericton, Boston, Manhattan, Brooklyn, Philadelphia, Montreal, Ottawa, Toronto, Hamilton, Chicago, Winnipeg, Calgary, Vancouver, Victoria, Seattle. Her publicist taught her how to order steak tartare and oysters from room service. Calls from a proprietor at CookeMcDermid, an agent from Transatlantic, and the housesit schedule fell to pieces. Before their faculty terms at the Banff Centre, they arranged matching workwear jackets from Vetra. Emily Haines put one of his lyrics to music, singing in mezzo-soprano with the Soft Skeleton. *No more traumas and penance in fiction*, they said. *It's time to give pleasures their due.*

In the acknowledgements of *Do I Do What I Want?*, she thanked the Scotiabank Giller Prize Board of Directors and the Giller Foundation Advisory Council. They flew to New York and back to Toronto and Chicago and back to Toronto in time for the Writers' Trust Storytellers Ball. She thanked Her Excellency the Right Honourable Governor General of Canada. They flew to Seattle and back and then to Boston and Montreal and San Francisco and Ottawa and Los Angeles, and finally back to Vancouver for the BC and Yukon Book Prize Gala. She thanked the trustees of the Griffin Poetry Prize. She thought eagerly of writing a one- or two-act play for Broadway. Samantha Hill in the solo performance. She thanked the Authors' Advisory Group of the Writers' Trust of Canada. She thanked the Writers' Trust Board of Directors and Ontario Creates' Program Director. Remembering the lines from Didion, she called the play *The Privilege Cops*. Then, thinking better of it, she called it *Sizes Zero and Two*.

# MEMORIAL PRAYER

PEOPLE LIKE TO say that after a death we feel the presence of the deceased—acutely, in the body, as a feeling and not merely as a wish. We believe in wild, magical dreams, like the dead are haunting us, lost, adrift, in need of our help. Later, after some months, nothing of this ghostly presence is left. The wave of feeling recedes; the tide calms and begins to lap. The gale becomes a breeze that, only now and then, lifts a hand to your face. That sense of continuity, of the dead just "hanging about"—simply the pain of our own habits, quashed. *You're supposed to be here. You're supposed to be lying exactly there, in the sun, on your bed. You're supposed to yawn and wake up.*

My habits are the same. I'm exactly as absurd. I used to feel, for instance, that if I went out for a walk, you'd think I was leaving you for good, that you'd be scared I wasn't coming back. *Oh, how inane,* I'd think—then indulge the thought, anyway. If I was in the garden, say, and heading inside at dusk, latching the gate behind me, I would feel you were still there, sentenced to spend the night alone, hunched against the bricks like some pitiful wretch. And while walking in the arbitrary city, the sidewalks empty, walking just to move, just to get outside the sunny house, I'd be scared you'd think it was permanent: some kind of grand exit, a pronouncement on finality. *This is an obvious absurdity.* Still, as I sold your bed, and packed away your toys, and took away the last bit of food and drink, I was worried you'd conclude there was no more place to rest, no more time for play, or nothing left to eat. And that was true—there was no more place to rest, no more time for play, and nothing left to eat, but not in the way I was thinking. I thought, preposterously, that when I leave this house for real, or when new faces appear, or when these walls come down and a new house is built, you'd think this was no longer home—that we were gone, and that you were not invited to come (which you weren't, literally. You could not be invited to come). I was careful not to hurt you then; you'd become powerless and tiny. So I didn't go back to the park, or to the school, or to the beach because I felt it would make you lonely—not to walk the broken string of stone and sand, scaring off the crying geese, not to spot the lighthouse splitting up from the rocky promontory, not to feel the lash and sting of the sulfurous lake. I thought you could hear me cough, or swear, or shuffle up the stairs. So I stepped lightly. It was like you were living just adjacent to me, or living because of me. I thought that you could hear me say things: *Christ, fuck it, please, goodnight.*

As time went by, I wondered, stupidly, if you could still feel the winds sweeping that memorial orchard we liked—the howling spells over the tarnished plaques, the faded names of the ignorant dead, the writhing corn fields and the sheer thrill of the heedless gusts. The shape of an animal, sudden on the rounded hill—a stag, a coyote, a horse!—and lungs hot, like blood in the mouth. Out of nowhere, I began to panic about where you were, and about your becoming. I thought maybe you were in a windy trench yourself, tossed by cravings you couldn't overcome, like Paolo or Francesca in a fictional landscape, trapped in a hurricane of your own making. So I thought I could direct you somewhere better with an enormous act of intention. I confess, I'd reached the depths of my absurdity. I actually sat and tried to guide your mind to that orchard, where you'd enjoy it there fully—running, drinking, sleeping, singing—for an eon, or thereabouts, and then one day, like waking up from a vivid dream, you'd recall it all perfectly, our afternoons and evenings, in the yard and at the beach, and you'd remember the lake, all the time that didn't exist, and you'd work at once without impediment to liberate us from our misery, wherever we were staying—in hell or some other hell. In awful absurdity, and for a full forty-nine days, I did this, beating a silly drum, breathing candle smoke and incense, chanting for the great and even greater compassionate ones to take pity on your helpless, rudderless heart.


Not much about being alive makes sense. It's like awareness. It's like dark matter and stigmata, like Zeno's arrow or rebirth, like the wave particle paradox or a clichéd cat in a box, neither living nor dead. No past, no future, but having one moment become the next, and then the next. Like hearing, from the World Honoured One himself, that while wandering on, for lo these many eons in lo these many arbitrary cities, that we've spilled more literal tears—over the loss of a mother, the loss of a father, the loss of a child, the loss of our husbands, the loss of our bodies—than there's water in the four great oceans. A ludicrous theory, but it was hard to think of anything else. I didn't tear my hair or wail. I didn't turn hard, mean or cruel, or just squash my feelings down and forget. I simply had the audacity, the temerity, to think I could help you out, which is what I was supposed to do. What kind of person does this? What kind of adult failure, or weakling, or fool?

These days, I feel nothing at all, except for now and then, when the wind lifts a hand to my cheek, and for those brief moments teeter on the edge of a crater, and then simply get back to work. The shore still laps at the beach, still roars over the stones, but I don't get wet. And neither do you. In the time you've been gone, the seasons moved—leaves in autumn, snow in winter, floods in spring, and another different, stranger summer—and all that seemed to come and perish was as absurd and hated and as dear and precious as a mirage. The seasons changed. That was not absurd; that was perfectly sound. It was frost and it was heat, it was light and it was dark. The mirage, too, was perfectly sound. So, too, was your beautiful body. So, too, was your beautiful body, even in its last arrangement of pain, under the cozy green blanket. Bobby, how absurd—I wanted a red alert for you. I wanted to send a high-frequency scan. I wanted to send a memorial prayer, as clear as an emergency broadcast, or a beacon sweeping the sea at night. I wanted to find you there, bobbing in waves of tears, and no longer alone, no longer lost, so relieved to see your daddy, you'd catch my line across the great ocean of birth and death. I actually thought this. In five years, I can't speak to it. In ten years, less. In twenty, thirty years, there might be only one thing left.

# THIS THING I BELIEVE

THIS THING I believe began as a gut feeling: a catch of throat-level revulsion after reading a really annoying tweet. Flickers of disgust, anger, that settled down to a stomach cramp—a haunt to ruin my dumb morning. Days later I would see the same thing repeated on related media. Not the exact same wording or syntax as the original tweet, of course, but with something of the same spirit. Enough to catch my attention and reignite my aversion. Enough to quietly wreck my day. This time I applied a few seconds of conscious attention to the way I was feeling and felt a corresponding increase, a spasm, in negative intensity. Oddly, I wanted to prolong this feeling. I wanted to prolong and magnify the pain I was feeling, to give it room to blossom, so I began combing through related media for echoes or variations of that original tweet. How it could be voiced with more bluntness or subtlety; how it could hurt and tease me in new, inventive ways. And here and there, a shard—brittle fragments needled together with invisible stitching born of my aversion, helping me thread a pretty convincing pattern. I was now pretty much convinced. What I mean is:

now my thoughts and feelings were moving together in covert fluidity toward something complicated and big. Now when I saw the painful thing repeated, my response didn't manifest as a gut feeling, a fleeting spasm. This thing I was feeling had now moulted into a thing I believe. Now it was a thing that was true, independent of my thinking. It had coalesced into a constellation, a rubric, a roadmap pointing toward more painful revelations, other forms of thinking. And the pain swelled in correspondence with my devotion; it discredited other things that other people loved and believed so that I became disgusted with those same rounded, glad-faced people. But it was also a source of dreamy pleasure, a pleasure made of subterranean concentration and of secret, gloating certainty. The pleasure of holding a dark, unruly promise, or something wretchedly, naggingly true. I now felt so energized in daydream and fantasy, so fired up by all this pain and pleasure, that I decided I should voice the thing I now believed to other people in germane and not-so-germane conversations as a way of challenging my rising confidence about the thing. I wanted to see if others could see what I saw, see if they themselves might accept the transfiguring power, the pleasure and pain, of a thing I believed, and soon consider it a thing they believed, too. Or rejected, which would mean I would return to the underground, deep-down, reddish-black pleasure of creating more convincing, harder-to-refute arguments in favour of that feeling, those impressions, now robust as a castle: a thing I believed. These encounters went happily, insofar as my interlocutors were not prepared to discuss the thing I believed with the same sophistication or rhetorical power because, of course, they had not spent the same amount of time thinking about it as I had. I was emboldened now to reach more people and set my goals at far more public, ambitious levels. There had grown a lonely ache inside me, a wish to see the thing I believed grow and take root beyond me. And I believed in the ache, believed in its painful way forward. Let us take it to Twitter, I thought. But I was careful not to ruin the thing I had spent so much time believing. I would present the thing I believe as pure information, not as a feeling, a thing I had felt in the gut and come to believe. Not me, specifically, because that would diminish the power of its universal evocations and reduce it to an advertisement for my dim-lit personality. It had to live alone, be itself an independent thing, an obelisk of its own standing. And sure, when others boosted and rallied around me, sharing the thing I believe, and while others arrayed themselves before me as noisome enemies to my thinking, I was for both camps of people at the very centre of the melee, but subtly—that was key. I was still the name-maker, still clearly the founder and the emblem of the truth or falsehood of the thing, depending on your perspective. And while the often-strident resistance I encountered did sometimes bum me out—at heart, I wanted everyone to believe the thing, wanted everyone to like me—having other people hate my thinking was also helpful. I convinced myself that having legit enemies was important to the truthiness of my thinking even as their barbs soared past my bulwarks and wounded whatever you might want to call the essential "me." Feeling myself threatened was thus inspiring, to say the least. Despite my desire for independence I had stitched this thing I believe into my own hollow and let the thing stand as a marker for who I am or might be: the kinds of friends I might hang out with and the people I might love or hate, the ways I'd spend my money and the things I'd eat. I'd let it stand in text, bio, homily, a harming trigger for those easily triggered by the thing I believe, no matter the consequences. It was with rare pleasure and pain that I was thus sorted psychically into tribes, allegiances, by way of the thing, now so much larger and darker, spinier and furrier, than those early impressions. So bold and cowlicked, like a child shifting on its own belly, that I felt parental: that my idea had grown and wormed from my slithering nest and made its own groping, writhing way in the world, flicking its tongue into the eyes and ears of other people. As weeks and months passed I could see my relationships change, sever, to the degree they aligned with this coiled, child-like, exterior-yet-interior thing, busy bending other people's ideas to its wet jaws and drumbeat. It was me, in its own way—the middle of me—so that if it were to be unwound or discounted by another destabilizing belief I would be facing something rather calamitous—at least personally. But I knew there was only one person capable of doing that grim, murderous work. I was safe if I wanted to be.

# OKAY

OKAY TO ANOTHER headache. Okay to sore eyes, exhaustion, the way your teeth never quite fit together even when at rest. Okay to the ache in the torn knee and the old broken wrist. Okay to the fear that the furnace won't turn on this February. Okay to the unanswered texts from your landlord, ignoring you from Kenya. Okay to your only pair of shit-brown eyes. Okay to the driving-test jitters and parallel parking with pep-pep. Okay to your sister's botched job interview, her plant-strewn apartment, her looming forties. Okay to the dog crying in the dark bedroom after his surgery. Okay to an itch, say; okay to the hint of a cold in an itch in the back of your throat. Okay to the word losing meaning: *okay*. Okay, this is okay. Okay to your mind right now, and now, and now, and now. Okay to clicking on YouTube videos teaching men about confidence from a channel called Charisma University. Okay to the pale rim of flesh around your waist you'll never burn away. Okay to this broken body, your broken body. Okay to bodies on top of each other, being gone soon, only a few more nights together. Okay to hopeless sleeping space forever. Okay to worms milling the frozen earth, your father's white face in the coffin. Okay to the dream of serial murderers wearing pink nightgowns with Michael Jackson's cat eyes from "Thriller." Okay to the dog's anesthesia wearing off, his sluggish licks, his thick trail of vomit. Okay to your panic. Okay. Okay to the meme you memorized from the other hateful tribe. Okay to the wish and the denial. Okay to spinach and kale, tomorrow. Okay to another list to make you productive, wake up at five in the morning and be better at your imaginary job. Okay to your mind right now, and now, and now in its cradle: a baby swallow in your hands, sealed eyes shivering, a monkey the size of a raisin covered in terrible bites. Okay to the monkey biting his own skin in the cramped cage and the stone bodhisattva statue shedding real tears. Okay to the LinkedIn summons. Okay to the gnashing of followers. Okay to the chill nimbus around the full December moon filling your mind with its angry spotlight. Okay. Okay to right now. Okay to anime robots with the faces of children flying along rainbows. Okay to spells, spell books, Toronto Waste Services and clapping garbage bins, the enraged woman you meet at Runnymede Station who speaks to herself in agitated whimpers. Okay to your phone saying it's time for bed. Okay to holding the dog under the blanket through the long February night. Okay to his small cries and to kissing his domed, fragrant head. Okay to the heater clicking on. Okay to the dog waking up and looking into your eyes.

V

# THE GATELESS GATE

After Mumon Ekai's Preface to *Mumonkon*

THEY SAY IT will be quick. They say it will be like catching a glimpse of a white horse galloping by your window: just as silly, just as bright. Or like catching a shooting star above you in cold space—a star or a satellite, or the International Space Station, or a twinkling rhomboid of rock—while you crane your neck to look. It will be your mother's silhouette, not one week dead, in the kitchen archway at 2:24 a.m., right before you throw on the oven light, go back to blubbering into sorbet. Someone's lucky hand in poker, flashed in drunken jest, and then the blurry afterimage: a few numbers, reds and blacks, the face of a queen or a jack. They say it will be like all these things. It will be the tip of the tongue, the top of the mind, a déjà vu, a quick goodbye—like a man hurtling past your office window from thirty floors up: a billow of cream-coloured coat, legs bent like in the tarot, and a blue September sky installed behind him. Before, you didn't notice a door. Up in the attic of nails, drywall, studs, and sour wallpaper, there were merely four walls, cobbling a room you'd come to know as yourself. Then it opened, and you remembered the dream from last night. You saw the fish surfacing and swallowing the silver fly. You saw the sun dart and dip to earth, as if to kiss, or drink. Before, you didn't even know there was a door. So when it closes again, just as quickly, it crushes your heart.

I was born a green acorn; my destiny, my job, is to become a scarlet oak. Born a wispy seed, I'll push through sticky, clumpy earth to unfurl my leaves. I was born a black mote to burst forth a tadpole. I'll grow muscular legs, become a frog, and sit very still, sucking flies in a murky bog, yum yum. Born a golden retriever, I'll run and bark and sleep in the sun until my eyebrows go white. Born a horse, I'll fall from my mother, but soon begin to trot. Born a man, my tongue turns to iron, my bones to dust. Unpacking boxes, opening cuts, rehearsing injuries in a dry, dusty attic, I spot the seam and groove and hinges of a door. I see the door open for the length of time it takes something bright to race past my window. Was that a white horse? Was it something as impossible, as magical? What is the one thing that nothing, no one, not one thing, has or can hold but me? With the baby robin, I *cheep-cheep* for my destiny. Sweating, finding sleep, waking, nodding off, rousing myself, slapping my cheeks, pacing, flopping down, drinking water, falling asleep again, unable to lift my chin, the radio static, the distorted waltz from rooms below me, heavy as lead, vinyl pop, falling asleep again.

Hilarious what the day devours. Hilarious to know, halfway through, that a year is something that eats. Finding a lack of choice in birth and subsisting. Letting things happen: letting chips fall where they may. All with a hilarious smile on my face. Months devour weeks. Years show themselves insatiable for the small, infinitely divisible things they contain. What's another nap in the warm attic? A slow clomp up the stairs to bed in the afternoon? What's another walk to the drugstore? What's another day spent hunting a password in an Excel file saved in a shared drive folder? A series of minute ethical decisions, like: did you feel bad for the red smear of rabbit on the highway? Did you respond with joy to your enemy's ascension? At the very end of the world, the very last night on earth, we go to bed. I mean to squeeze your hand all night. I mean to stay up, alert. But look at us—we've fallen asleep. Instead of holding or whispering through the crickets and sirens of this last summer night, we turn away, soon uncomfortable from the heat, and you sleep on your back, and I sleep on my right, the way I did as a child, cheek against a cool pillow. There's a twenty-five-year-old episode of *The Simpsons* flashing pink and blue and yellow over our dreaming heads, beamed from the light of a laptop on the bed. At one point in the night, still asleep, I sit up. I point toward the wall where, for a moment, there is a door.

# YES AND NO

THERE IS NO place called "Starbucks Coffee." There is no wan dream of high school, no red-and-gold players in the long, glossy halls. There is no fixed number of precepts, nor signposts for you to follow, and no reclaimed barnwood gone bad on the sideroad. There is no Irish setter, lost in the moody gulch, purple posters marked with Sharpie flapping wetly in the dusk. And there is no cubic cannabis dispensary on the main drag, nor a Domino's and Papa Johns, no Circle K and its field of empty Pepsi bottles, tossing and

THERE IS A place called "Starbucks Coffee." There is a wan dream of high school, of red-and-gold players in the long, glossy halls. There is a fixed number of precepts, signposts for you to follow, and a piece of reclaimed barnwood gone bad on the sideroad. There is an Irish setter lost in the moody gulch, purple posters marked with Sharpie flapping wetly in the dusk. And there is a cubic cannabis dispensary on the main drag, a Domino's and Papa Johns, a Circle K and its field of empty Pepsi bottles, tossing turning in thirst. There is no toddler warbling from a stroller, no set of hand-me-down wheels, no mother stalking in Lycra, and no nimbus clouds or barometric pressure, so no migraine to match. No WhatsApp alert from Southampton makes a soft chirrup in your pants. There is no silent airbus in a sky half-pillaged of stars. There is no degenerative arthritis, no squirm or stiffness in the knee, and no person who socked you in the kisser. No underwater traffic shushes from Liberty Street, and no incense burns the nostrils: white sage and cedar. No sense of a time before, nor a time after—no alphabet soup of oblivion, no flash of pink from *The Croods* on a little boy's iPad. No social update, no kill-yourself mantra, no beloved's psoriasis in late-day Alzheimer's: no tongue dabbed with water when she couldn't drink herself. There is no Giant Tiger and no Dollarama. There are no teenaged lovers on the library's

and turning in thirst. There is a toddler wailing from a stroller, a set of hand-me-down wheels, a mother stalking in Lycra, and some nimbus clouds and barometric pressure that will make a migraine appear. A WhatsApp alert from Southampton makes a soft chirrup in your pants. There is a silent airbus in a sky half-pillaged of stars. There is degenerative arthritis, a squirm and stiffness in the knee, and a person who socked you in the kisser. Underwater traffic shushes from Liberty Street, and incense burns the nostrils: white sage and cedar. A sense of a time before, a time after—an alphabet soup of oblivion, a flash of pink from *The Croods* on a little boy's iPad. A social update, a kill-yourself mantra, your beloved's psoriasis in late-day Alzheimer's: her tongue dabbed with water when she couldn't drink herself. There is a Giant Tiger and a Dollarama. There is a pair of teenaged lovers on the library's second floor, holding each other's faces. There is no midnight train whistle and foggy throat rattle, no cloud of carbon monoxide nor wan dream of high school, those red-and-gold players in the long, glossy halls. There is no place called "Starbucks Coffee." There is no inside or outside, no green light or finish. There is no person calling your name, no living thing you let go: there's nothing that will never come back.

second floor, holding each other's faces. There is a midnight train whistle and foggy throat rattle, a cloud of carbon monoxide and a wan dream of high school, those red-and-gold players in the long, glossy halls. There is a place called "Starbucks Coffee." There is an inside and an outside, a green light and finish. There is a person calling your name, a living thing you let go: there is something that will never come back.

# TURN YOUR ANGER INTO SADNESS

SO YOU'VE BEEN unfollowed. *So You've Been Publicly Shamed.* So: a good friend's wedding reception passes in October and all your lovers crowd under the Perpetua filter—the best one. So a good friend's Facebook profile turns to a grey silhouette, or spectre, and then is gone (and where did you go, oh pockmarked Josh of 2001, your frosted hair and Fox Racing fullback cap? I wanted to catch up, poke around, and now all I have is a BMX, the silver sizzle of you at the Warped Tour, mouth open, moshing to The Used). An acquaintance dies from heart failure, his obit pic dredged up from high school. So you haven't spoken in years, but still, you can't forget, or forgive, that he unfollowed you in December. And more friends attend his cottage funeral, where someone plays Blink-182's "First Date" on a Yamaha (or so you hear). So you've been unfollowed, and each time it happens, someone's found your hidden worms; someone's grabbed your blackened, blistered heart. So Hotmail got all glitchy, all of a sudden, back in 2007, and then all your ex's emails vanished—a whoosh into the Realm of Emptiness—but you still have your uptight replies from 2008. *I never said that*, you wrote, in a dream of a letter. *I'd never say that to anyone.* So you sound so shitty arguing with, having your chest ripped up by, The Void. So this subtweet is about you, and isn't. So: this is a code, or subtext—this is a pile-on, a witch hunt, some of that good ol' mob justice. So no one thinks about you for longer than thirty seconds, ever, unless they're gossiping, and in the presence of Jesus, or worried about your opinion, or they're getting off. So now you care about all the small things, now your FOMO haunts your no-shows, now your late-night scrolls through a few thousand faces asks the same two questions: who's still following, who's still got your back? So *Is Shame Necessary?* and I think you know the answer. So *I Thought It Was Just Me.* So *Radical Self-Acceptance.* So "regret" is kaukritya and either unwholesome or changeable but always a hindrance to those who've been canned, to those taken off the air. So your anger, there—there!—is breaking up into sadness; the hot bag of blood comes juddering out, painting the perfect white bed sheets. So now you're working on it hardcore, like you're whipping flour, like kneading cold clay in sore hands. It's what you're supposed to be doing: turning your anger into sadness, because anger has wrecked your accounts, because sadness hurts fewer people. You think of moraines snapped from glaciers. You think of a huge icy knife, all chopped up. So you've been unfollowed en masse—you've been officially deplatformed. So your acquaintance, once a good friend, almost exactly yourself, and now a tight bag of ashes, once stood beside you in grade school, Velcro-to-Velcro, on the low wooden bench, posing for a class photo, hearts thudding like swallows, arms as thin as laptop screens. Both of you smiling into a future that got cancelled. So, instead of saying sorry forever, you think of proud Niobe and her brood of murdered children. Where, even as the Weeping Rock, mum and bored to death, she only stains herself.

# IN THE 2000s

*In tribute to Leonard Michaels (1933–2003)*
*and to Joe Brainard (1942–1994)*

THE 2000S BEGAN for me in the basement of my parents' friends' bungalow. I was forced to spend the evening with their son, whom I barely
knew, and my sister, who was five years younger and so only ten years
old. By the time the countdown came around I had drunk a few glasses
of warm brandy and felt buzzed and giddy for the first time in my life. I
danced alone to "Funky Town" in the light of a strange television screen
and thought, *Thank you, God, for sparing us from Y2K.*

For most of the 2000s I had long hair and a skeletal frame. I was so skinny
you could see my organs pulsating beneath my skin, but that didn't stop
me from smoking until my fingers turned yellow, or drinking until I woke

with torn ligaments, black eyes, a blistered throat. Drinking was a great virtue. All the most important things happened to us because of alcohol.

I had an argument with my reflection one night, high on absinthe in a bathroom at a Soviet-themed bar. The taps gleamed in the murky lights, and the bartenders were gorgeous, red-haired Russian intellectuals. We spoke about poetry and music long after last call and until we were forced to leave.

In the 2000s there was much at stake between friends. In chronological order, I lived with my mother, father, sister, three friends across Europe, a whole floor of people at the University of Ottawa, then three friends, then one, then six at once, then two others, then two more. You got used to having strange guests, parties, hearing people through the walls fighting, crying, having sex. You assumed you would know these people for the rest of your life. You knew what their cryptic MSN Messenger statuses meant.

I had a girlfriend who lost herself in dreams about miracles and Jesus; who scratched her face raw and turned all her books backward, said she could see angels dancing in the rafters of Saint Paul University and tried to crawl out my bedroom window to fall to her death. I still have a wooden rosary she gave me from Medjugorje, where the Virgin gives out little stones to fell your Goliath (viz., Satan). One night, I crawled into bed with her and wept about heaven. Late in our relationship, a nun, visiting her Catholic parents in Peterborough, told them I was "a bum" based purely on my name—a feeling she got about me. By the end of it my girlfriend said we would end up in Azkaban (the prison from the Harry Potter franchise) if we stayed together, meaning we'd have gone insane together. I found this idea romantic. When she dumped me, I lay in bed feeling pinned through the chest by a flagpole. She was not crazy, but full of pearly wisdom. I then entered a long emotional phase and listened to a lot of depressing music on my iPod touch.

In the 2000s I got excellent grades at the University of Ottawa then University of Toronto by believing that they mattered to my eventual fruition (like a lotus blooming in mud), that I would be a professor or scholar, editor or writer. A magazine man, or something. My professors were mythic, Titan-like figures—icons, saints, objects of ridicule, rogues and adventurers—and to impress them I disgraced myself again and again.

When our family dog died—when she spasmed, had a stroke, was put down at the age of thirteen—and I heard the news from my parents, I was surprisingly unaffected. I was more uncomfortable hearing my dad's weepy voice on the telephone, telling me what had happened. Later, looking through photos of our dog on Facebook, I said my goodbye: a sudden sob that sounded just like a scream. My roommate rushed downstairs in terror, but I played it off, saying it was just an extremely forceful sneeze.

I swam in the English Channel at Dieppe, kissed a German girl on a school trip in Strasbourg, caught a horrific fever in Amsterdam, lost my euros on trains across France, sweated and scoured the cobbles of Florence for spare change, read *Leaves of Grass* and underlined a passage on every page, rode alone through the Alps toward Munich, and there chanted "yes" in the streets at midnight, crying "yes" to everything—everything was on its way.

We marched in protest when George W. Bush visited Ottawa. We marched over and over, against the Conservatives, amid the drums and chants and sear of tear gas, carrying home-made signs. Mine read, "There is a spectre haunting Ontario," which I thought was very clever. Mounted police charged us in Toronto and eventually hit us with bicycles. I didn't believe we were just moving chairs on the Titanic. We were thrilled to see fences ripped down, great masses of people gathering at Queen's Park and Parliament Hill, even though the crowds represented far, far fewer than one percent of the cities' populations. Old women wore woolen bonnets, and one woman, a Trotskyite, had a full-blown moustache, which I thought was magnificent. Rows of businessmen would watch us from glass towers and balconies, smoking, and laugh and laugh.

I worked in the produce department at a place called Marilu's Market, as a dishwasher at Lakeshore Place Retirement Home, a lighting technician at Living Lighting, a clerk at Dowsar Yachts & Marine Supplies, a dry cleaner at Market Cleaner's, a TA at the University of Toronto, and as a desk receptionist at Global Village Backpackers Hostel in Kensington Market. I tutored dozens of ESL university students and the occasional frail Portuguese boy in high school doldrums, and once, two tiny French-Lebanese sisters in Gatineau, where I was served sugar cookies and honeyed tea and cigarettes. Aside from the tedium, injuries, and drip-drop paycheques, all my memories of work are of smoke breaks, reading breaks, writing breaks, dread. Looking out the windows at dawn and dusk, eating fast food, waiting for sexy customers, dreaming about art and the future—lost in my own boredom and impotence.

I saw a ghost in my parents' basement in Burlington, Ontario, around 2006. At home with them over the summer, one night before falling asleep in my subterranean bedroom, I opened my eyes to see a black shadow of a man standing over me, making a silent accusation: a finger shoved into my face.

My first girlfriend and I broke up in the summer of 2003, right before I went off to university. We were together for maybe six months. She was letting me down gently, knowing I was going away on a great journey and we wouldn't want to be tied down to one another. We were lying in a playground park that night, which I remember as foggy and unseasonably cool, and we shared her hoodie for a pillow. It was for my own good, but I would have stayed with her forever had she asked me. I can still see her walking home in September, in the streetlight, before I walked home myself.

My grandfather died suddenly—a bad stomach ache, then cancer, then *poof.* He listened to Willie Nelson's *Stardust* on my portable CD player in the slate-blue hospital by the lake. At the age of seventeen, I kissed his forehead in his sour-smelling bed. I was reminded, then, of Aragorn kissing Boromir in *The Fellowship of the Ring.* Some time during the dying and grieving process, I watched my mom cry while eating Pizza Hut delivery.

The first time I rode the subway in Toronto, trucking from Dundas West Station to St. George, from my home on Alhambra Avenue to the University of Toronto, I was delirious with excitement, like a child at an amusement park, finally given a go-ahead to ride the roller coaster for big kids, even though I was already twenty-five, a mild alcoholic, and registering for graduate school.

In the 2000s I stayed up all night and watched the sun come up a handful of times. Probably like, twelve times, maximum. I felt as though important and soulful people were supposed to stay up and watch the dawn, so I did, feeling sick with fatigue.

In the 2000s I earned and lost my driver's licence. To get around, I rode buses and subways and trains and, for a brief summer in Ottawa, a bicycle. I walked thousands of kilometres on my ruined knee. One night I was howling at the top of my lungs and fell asleep in a snowbank, in a snowstorm, as the temperature dropped to minus thirty. Suicide was a possibility; I had just given up. I missed the girl who saw the angels and saved us from Azkaban. A passing ambulance saved my life!

I tried to study English literature in Galway, Ireland, on an exchange program with the University of Ottawa. It would be a year-long trip. I was a shoo-in with my excellent grades and references, but I got stupid drunk on shots of dark rum on the morning of an exchange meeting and was kicked out of the program by the coordinator. I would have been a terrible representative for the school, she said.

I took care of a girlfriend's black cat while she was away in Botswana, in 2010, doing something related to social work and HIV. This cat was nasty to everyone, would bite and claw and yowl. But while I was out of the apartment she would wail and beg for me, tormenting my roommates, who'd demand that I come home and comfort her. I'd walk through the doorway after work and scoop her up into my arms, tsking, rocking her like a baby, cooing into her fur, her heartbeat slowing, her yellow eyes locked to mine like a first-time lover. She'd lie on my feet at night, kneading me with her claws. After the relationship ended, my ex-girlfriend's father arrived to pick up the cat after months of delays—and I tossed her into her carrier with a single throw.

I started a literary magazine that angered dozens of people involved in publishing in Ottawa and embarrassed myself in excruciating, unforgettable ways until the magazine got a little better, a bit more competent, but by that time I was leaving the city and the whole thing folded, later to be resurrected online. But all the ads we sold to local businesses, all the stores we got to sell the mag by commission, all the work we did on the childish website or the readings we organized: no one remembers those things. The festival events, selling in gymnasiums, talking to small-press harpies and putting on airs like I actually knew something. This magazine ended or prevented several friendships, but at the time seemed like the most important mission, a spotlight from heaven, saying, "Here is the way forward," and it was, for a while.

In the 2000s I became enamored of my English teacher, who, starting at the age of twenty-seven—a decade older than me—taught me through grades

11, 12, and 13, and stoked my desire to read poems and write them. He was a desperately sensitive, sad person, and if he let you into his secret world of turbulent emotion and clandestine affairs you felt chosen—lambent. And I tried desperately to impress this person; for a time, he was my father and god. I was jealous of his other friends, his girlfriends. I would email and write to him, I'd pore over his inscrutable handwriting, and we would have drinks together through the 2000s, in waning frequency. Though I dream about him every few months, I recall only a few scattered things he said to me, now, by way of advice. "You carry yourself wherever you go," he said, which is kind of like Jon Kabat-Zinn's *Wherever You Go, There You Are*. "You're no longer my student, but just another man I know," which is a way of saying, "Leave me alone already."

In the 2000s I used to sit at the back of churches and cry, silently, during Mass, in my absurd leather jacket, and then go home to eat canned stew and masturbate.

We would butcher music together at parties in high school. We would practice our instruments in my parents' basement before they renovated, meaning the concrete walls destroyed my ear drums: an irreversible decision from the 2000s that has meant near-incessant tinnitus. Soon I gave up my electric guitar and focused on picking my way through acoustic folk and country. I used to sing to myself, and sometimes to girls I was "dating" or trying to impress. I would fantasize about creating a country cover band, playing bars that would have us, and be accompanied by a violinist and pedal steel guitar. I came close on a few occasions to putting that band together, but you can't fake real talent, and now I'm relieved it never happened.

In the 2000s I was pinned to the wall by pop music. I'd listen to the same songs over and over, like scratching a bite. Pop singers became my girl-friends. Life was lived behind a gorgeous red veil. One song would make me brave. I'd sit to write something after listening to pop, full of manic energy, and come away empty-handed. No poem or novel could touch those major chords, the ravishing faces, the staging of misery. YouTube slew me. There in the underground pool hall in Ottawa, earbuds in, while my friends wore masks like Muses of Comedy. My portable CD player, skipping tracks, head-phones on, riding the Greyhounds across Ontario. This year, I found a mix CD from a friend from 2007, inserted it into my car's CD player, but hit eject before the first song began. Instead of listening I threw it into the garbage.

I used, in order, a Dell Inspiron, a loaned desktop, an old eMac, then a refurbished MacBook, in the 2000s. I used dozens of floppy disks, an email account with the University of Ottawa and the University of Toronto, a Hotmail account and a Gmail account. I had ICQ, MSN Messenger, MySpace, Twitter, and Facebook. I had a Nikon cellphone, countless flip phones, and Android smartphones. I used six or seven separate landlines. I still remember my phone number from grade 1 all the way up to 2003: 634.5491 rattled off in a sing-song lilt. My first email address, maintained through-out the 2000s, was rex_cobo69@ hotmail.com. I created this at the age of thirteen, and aside from the obvious number, it references a porn star I saw in a glossy magazine ad—"Rex Cobo: The Man with the Elastic Scrotum."

In the 2000s, Burlington, the suburban place where I grew up, changed from an irradiated pit of boredom, badlands of strip malls and concrete, to something sublime in memory, never to be recaptured, always to be chased, until it slipped through my fingers completely. The last stretch of time I spent there was the summer of 2008. My parents were travelling. I was housesitting in August, alone with our family dog and the ghost in the basement. I'd sit on the cold ground in our crawl space surrounded by photo albums and red wine, VHS tapes and pentagrams, a Ouija board peering at me from a shelf of board games I'd played with my little sister when we were kids. I'd pound out songs on our out-of-tune piano and the dog would sleep with me, curled into the crook of my knees, warm in bed. Everything had changed within those ten years. Everyone had moved away, and no one was coming home. This feeling would possess me for another decade and then fade to a memory, a dream of a disappointment, something you can't change so stop bothering to try.

My friend Ben staged, faked, his own death. Everyone was cut up and devastated, thinking he had fallen at a military camp during basic training, and had died at twenty-two or twenty-three. His funeral was being planned in Burlington. People bought plane tickets home. Turned out it was all a strange joke. His girlfriend had posed as his mother, answering tender telephone calls from friends. That was the last time anyone saw him. He moved immediately after the ruse was discovered and was never seen again. So, in a way, he was successful.

I don't remember how the 2000s ended.

In the early 2000s I wore thrift-store shirts and shoes, tiny T-shirts, flared denim patched up a dozen times by the surly but lovable Vietnamese seamstress in the dry cleaners where I worked. I wore a leather jacket whittled away to threads and crooked aviator sunglasses. By the end of the decade I was wearing skinny jeans, beanie caps, things with ironic brand names or grotesque faces, and Ray-Ban sunglasses. V-necks. Cheugy, now. But nothing I wore still exists. It has all decomposed and returned to the earth.

During one summer I took the GO Train to see yet another girlfriend who was living during June, July, and August in Mississauga, Ontario. We would fight like bloodied horses, biting off each other's ears, hooves and teeth colliding mid-air. She had no interest in anything I liked; I don't remember her liking anything at all, in fact. There was no reason we were together. But I would write her preposterous letters and love poems, my penmanship screwy with each bump of the train. I felt so bad, so hopeless when the relationship ended, that I had to see a doctor. My stomach, groin, and hips were in torment. It was all an enormous muscle spasm. Self-induced, the doctor said. It went away, but every now and then, even today, it comes back as if it never left.

In the 2000s I wrote a novella that took me a year and half to write. I got halfway through a novel that took me three years to fail at. I completed maybe fifteen short stories and about a hundred poems. I wrote a stack of essays that, printed, stood three feet off the ground; I filled at least the same amount in notebooks for school and pleasure. I wrote in the light of laptop screens at night and would get into my broken single bed while my struggling Inspiron was still shutting down. It would take about twenty minutes to power-off completely, buzzing and churning like an old dog circling its bed before finding sleep. I loved to lie under the covers in that glow, comforted, having the day finally draw down and night come on, waiting for the blue screen to go black. Feeling like *good things are coming if only I can hold out a bit longer*. Feeling like life was still long, and an adventure. Feeling like even if it wasn't, even if it was all going to shit, I had *tried*, at the very least. So comforted, in fact, that I'd try to fight the first pull of sleep, bathed in that underwater blue, by trying to remember everything that happened to me—that day, week, month, even year. I was always forgetting something. There was always something happening, *right now*, right here in the 2000s, I had to hold on to, to write down in blood. I couldn't let it slip away, let it be lost to sleep and convenience, in the last night of my youth. I'd soon be packing boxes again; I'd soon be leaving town. I'd soon be waving goodbye, and it would feel like another temporary pause, a droll wink from a U-Haul, a disconnect on a long-distance call, but this time it would last forever. Trying to remember, I'd watch the moon become so bright and large that it would fill my window and then the entire sky. Shining, my eyes would soon see and reflect only that white light—soft and pure as a peony, or a calla lily, or a carnation. Soon that light would be the total horizon. Soon, my eyes full of flowers, I would remember everything perfectly.

# THERE IS NOTHING TO DISLIKE

After Línjì Yìxuán (d. 866 CE)

*"If you are feeling sorry for yourself, you should be ashamed."*
—Shunryū Suzuki (1904–1971), quoted by Marion Derby (1923–2013)

NO MORE PROFILES, hot takes, or mentions. How can I annotate a dahlia? I haven't seen you in forever, yet here we are, back together, draining a bucket of red wine in a redwood shack. A small, warm room in the woods, faces aflame with shadow and light, while snow lies three feet deep on the pines, and animals—the poor animals!—quiver on the branches. Eventually, it's all you can do to shut up and die, to snap the lips closed for good, and if a bullet comes whizzing over the Wi-Fi, why gripe? Falling away, you hear a perfect chord and melody. When will the plague arrive? When's the Big One coming? When will I retire? Where is my only daughter? Still, we sit and complain, stretching long, skinny legs toward the fire. Teeth red and yellow, crooked in the flicker. Adding petals to medicinal hours. Warming the stars with woolen socks. Ringing the snowy mountains with hoary adornments of pine and, full of grief, falling asleep with gymnastic, balletic technique. In my dreams, you and I are nineteen. We are walking in Florence, crossing a bridge in the fever of July—memory's bridge, memory's Florence—speaking words that have departed, that do not exist any longer, and we are both crying with wonder to be saying them all over again. The summer clouds appear in the water—rounder than mirrors, sharper than thorns, hotter than heaven. Beneath it the streams flow on in the buried darkness, seen in a vision without sight. Now, there is nothing to dislike, I think—and so it all vanishes. No shack, no wine. No perfumed memory. No stars. No me. No you.

# THE FIRE SERMON

SOME PEOPLE ARE eunuchs. Some people become eunuchs through happenstance, hormone, accident, or trauma, and there are some people who make themselves eunuchs for the Holy Spirit. Jesus says this in the Gospel of Matthew, more or less. He also says, in the Sermon on the Mount, that it's better to pluck a malfunctioning eyeball from your own head—to lose, and burn, a priceless member—than it is to blink your whole body, stumble-down drunk, into hell.

In this spirit, it's rumoured that Origen of Alexandria—prolific exegete, tortured believer, vegetarian, and apologetic—had a surgeon lop off his genitals to head off claims of impropriety with his mixed-sex students. Better to be castrated than risk a loss of respect, one might assume. Or better to sever ties with sensation than have six inches of flesh get you cancelled—or burned. Or so claimed Eusebius in the *Ecclesiastical History*, but now we know this is probably fake news.

We are talking about an elementary process: losing a particle to save the whole. Fires have their natural function; each regime has a cadence and purpose. One part burns away, and another is born. Clicking on what's trending by the hour, we learn about fires, their elegance and mercies, the smudged-lens focus on an annihilated township. Trees expire to sustain the forest; branches are pruned to save the tree. Pressed, we might consider this a metaphor for body and soul. So King Nebuchadnezzar, destroyer of nations, can toss you into a Babylonian prison cell and threaten you with death. Because you won't kneel to him—he who is King of the Universe, King of Totality—he's going to throw you headlong into a furnace. And because you believe in the cadence of fire, the char and the metaphor, you can just say *nah*, I won't forsake the Lord. Throw me into the flames. Make me a sheep and serve me raw to starving lions. Go ahead, for what you put to death is only that which is earthly in me. The dross, the flesh, the dust, the dead. That which feeds the worm and the olive and the million mouths of weeds.

A bonfire of the vanities heads off an occasion to sin and most likely proximate. Hard to give up. Habitual. Cherished. A rope to lariat the hell-bound heart. Girolamo Savonarola, Dominican friar, preacher and firebrand, saw mirrors, makeup, flutes, jewellery, and works of irreplace-able Renaissance genius—Botticelli, Boccaccio—as all serving the same secular purpose. Like a game of dice gone bad and an outstanding loan, goons ready to toast your ankles under a Romanesque arch. Like a little polished mirror in which your face goes from smooth and rose, Olivia Rodrigo, to wan and ruined, Clint Eastwood, all in an orgasm, semen on skin, candle-lit in the cell of a sex worker in Florence who is owned body and soul by the Onestà. Today, Marie Kondo tells mortal vessels, itching for improvement, that most things we own are detractions. Most things, it seems, are part of the regimen of fire. But how to know what to keep? How to know what to leave? Hold things close, she says, and if they spark joy, they stay. If they don't, they burn, but with gratitude, a quiet thank-you-for-your-service. Savonarola was hanged and burned in a piazza now crowded with tourists and pigeons, commerce and selfie-sticks, and if he felt that a locket or a painting or a poem sparked joy, it was better to throw it into a bonfire than have it lure you, as if by the nose, into a fire that does not go out. Despite their karmas, both Kondo and the friar would agree: nothing survives this passage but a skull, and a skull soon enough becomes dirt. The wise and happy learn to snuff the flame, unclench the fist.

T. S. Eliot could not unclench. He saw the end of an era, based purely on his imagination, on the banks of the Thames. Conjuring Spenser and Wagner, Psalm 137, Verlaine, Baudelaire and Shakespeare, St. Augustine, and *The Parliament of Bees*, he asks us to despise the sludge of rain-soaked riverbanks, the stench of garbage and bureaucrats, of chips stands and cigarettes. He valorizes Parsifal—*Parsifal!*—who vanquished Hell by spurning a horde of lascivious women. He reminds us of Philomela, estranged into a nightingale, and he stands in horror of the homosexual, suggesting a casual hookup. Today, Eliot would roil with incel energy: aghast at a vision of Grindr, adrift in the eddies of a Hot Girl Summer. Oh, meaningless jobs, empty fucks, sexual violence through the papier-thin divider, the demotic and the cucked. The horror, the horror. But Eliot's project is all sublimation. We imagine him standing in the swirl of a London winter, wet clumps of snow soaking through his bank-clerk best, on the steps of a party to which he was emphatically not invited. Inside, all his fur-coated, cheese-breathed friends and a refrigerator full of jingling champagne. The warm lights, the ASMR murmur, the lols and gramophone crackle, the rooms, and the coming and the going, and I am alone. I am losing my mind in a rainy, dreadful country. I can say this in Greek and Latin, French and Italian and German, and I am completely unloved. Burning. Burning. The Lord plucketh me. Burning.

In artist KC Green's "On Fire," a six-panel webcomic from 2013 CE, a yellow dog wearing a hat sits at a table and sips a mug of coffee. Flames roar around him. Smoke obscures the ceiling. The room is burning, burning, burning. By the fourth panel, so is he. "This is fine," the dog says, with a smile, adorable googly eyes. "That's okay, things are going to be okay." According to the artist, the dog "melts into nothingness" while smiling angelically. The strip seems to ask: how can you cope with the world's appalling injustice, the Jenga-stacked tragedies, when there are papers to grade, cranes to operate, managers to appease, wailing kids to feed? Then it answers: hope endures, automatically, in a dumb affirmation, spouted by dying celebrities, celebrity presidents, by roasting forests, thawing icecaps. The end of the world will be endured in any mood, any attitude, so we might as well smile while we melt.

We are far from finding a part that endures. We are far from grasping an I, a me, a mine, even as we hold our pronouns close, hoping they sparkle with joy. What I grasp burns me, horribly. It disfigures my radiant skin. It poisons me against my friends. Like taking up a ball of iron from a furnace and swallowing it whole. Like embracing an anvil while the pein hammer wails. What I see is earthly. What I hear is earthly. What I taste is earthly. What I feel with this peeling, blistered skin is earthly. And what I remember is earthly. What I think, and dream, is earthly—here in Babylon, here in Florence, here in Alexandria, here in Galilee. So what is left? How can I pluck the eye? From what am I plucked? What can I cut away to save, and what inspires gratitude? What furnace can I step into and not be dissolved? What cannot be dissolved? What is the one thing that cannot be dissolved? It is impossible to say just what I mean.

In Albanian, the word for Thursday is "e enjte," which came roiling out of the name for Enji, the Illyrian god of fire—a deity of vital importance across the western Balkans for many blissful growth cycles. In the north, there was the fire god Verbt, whose name emerged from "vorbull"—a whirlwind, or vortex. Both Enji and Verbt got demoted to demon status when Christians came along in the fourth century and got cooking after the Byzantine missionaries. In the same-ish regions we have Nëna e Vatrës, goddess of the hearth, in which the souls of ancestors would mingle and scheme over all things domestic. If we trace things back to Indo-European roots, and it seems we must, Enji pays homage to Agni: the flaming-haired, two-faced, many-tongued god of fire in Vedic myth. And though he has no devoted sect, men still practice Agnihotra up to this moment to be absolved of evils—men who watch the home fires morning and night, tending the hearth, feeding the flames, dripping libations of milk, seeds, and ghee, and sending up oily wisps of immortality. The average resident of Southern Ontario would find it absurd to ascribe a spiritual dimension to a fireplace, even one containing authentic, crackling wood. This same Netflix, Prime, or Crave subscriber would scoff at any whiff of the sacred in the mundane. They would laugh at worshipping a literal god of fire. Like all gods before Christ, the gods of fire and hearth are now cartoon characters, or lavishly depicted in the Marvel Cinematic Universe. A slightly more sophisticated air traffic control attendant or high school drama teacher in the Halton, Ontario, region might retract this snub by suggesting that all gods are merely emanations of the mind, even and especially those that ruin our hopes. And who are we to judge, we with our tax-exempt cathedrals, synagogues, and mosques, and our doorways smeared with bloody handprints, and the news tolling on about beheading and circumcisions and doom. Another sort of person, slightly more sophisticated than the previous—say an author of fantasy novels, say an optometrist—might take us back through historical realism to the time of the Illyrians, and imbue the city of Epidamnus with the stink of an open marketplace, of dirt-caked coins pressed into calloused palms for tethered goats, all bleating for a salvation that wouldn't come. Or the city of Daorson at dawn, riveted by shadows cut by its megalith defences. To do so would also inject a romantic veneer upon the polytheistic and archaic and coax the reader to imagine the legit majesty of seeing the sun, the moon, or a simple flame—or even the humble family hearth—as bearing a terrible, alien, comforting significance. As if a flame's origin was indeed unearthly—coming out of nothing, arriving with magnificent energy, a noble visitor to the earth. To imagine the synchronicity of phenomena, a sensible cause and effect, and not a tangle of heaps and broken images, as with Eliot fondling the medieval pyramid in imagination, built as a bulwark against his personal misery. A yet more sophisticated interpretation of those rosy-fingered dawns, long before the advent of penicillin or lightbulbs, might take root in a Canadian fond of charcuterie boards or Muskoka lodges, and deepen her profound-but-never-voiced sadness for an entire people who walked into the inferno and never returned, whose language was buried in ash. A sadness not for their small struggles and dreams (or not only for them, not only for these lost whimpers and bellows) but to note that the flame of life back then, in the 600s and 700s of the "Before Common Era," was just as hot as it is today, in a Kia Sportage in a drive-thru Tim Hortons, idling in the lineup, waiting to place an order for cream and sugar, a bit of reassuring dark roast, a miniature but crucial pleasure, and a way to make the day shifts less cruel. Perhaps more sophisticated would be the drive-thru attendant at the same Timmies, wearing a visor, headset, and collared uniform, who might simply ask through the distorted speakers: "Why is it sad to imagine a people gone forever, buried by a million fires and new growths, and what, deeper, is really at the root of our longing for difference, longevity, testimony, when the earth is hotter than ever and seems more lost every summer?" What is the religious impulse even in the most tragic and husked, in the universe growing so steadily obese that soon flames from far-flung galaxies will never reach our miserable eyes? And to save it, we aren't willing to husk even our tiny, insignificant subscriptions, to cut a piece away to save the whole. And another Hyundai Venue passenger, idly playing with the automatic locks in her own vehicle in the same lineup for sugary snacks, might feel it odd to express any superiority over those who worshipped flames when she herself cannot recall what fire is: she literally Wikipedias the term "fire" on her Motorola and finds words and phrases there she has never heard spoken and has never, and will never, quite understand. And even if she did comprehend the "frequency spectrum" and "blackbody radiation" and "photon emission" mentioned in the most cursory articles, she would still flick her two-inch Bic to produce the most curious, indescribable thing: a licking magic, a sparkling warmth, a danger, a marvel, a freak-out, and know these words are more true, in an odd way, than our clean definitions of matter. She would know they are more akin to the language of those who speak of the sublime, like a minister she had as a child, or the imam on the Arabic channel, or the spiritual books she herself has scoffed at written by the likes of Eckhart Tolle or Deepak Chopra, she's not stupid. Behind her in the underpass, lying under stock-still tent canvas, is a homeless man named David, with a homeless man's clichéd, twisted beard and long, dirty locks, and he, too, understands that he will never understand, and that even those precise scientific terms we just trotted out are part of a faith, part of a cloister and ritual, and not really fire. He feels deeply troubled by this, and not in small measure because a fire took his home as a boy, began his family's limp into destitution, and ineluctably led him here to this sweating tent near the Tim Hortons drive-thru. And David knows there are physicists out there who know far better than even he does that the terms used collectively to refer to the spectrum of light, the fuel source, the functioning and extinguishing of flame, etcetera, are simply stabs in the dark, and shouldn't be clung to, for they will be surpassed by better evidence sporting different titles in the not-too-distant future, when we may know or see far more than we do today and thus require a different set of eyes (or a different tongue): perhaps through new treatments to grow new organs or graft onto our bodies new windows to the vast, limitless world. And perhaps there is a lady in Southern Ontario who, completely losing her sense of self, completely lost to a dream she had, somehow worships Enji in her own crooked way. And maybe this lady is not so lonely, and maybe she builds great pyres of garbage in her backyard in Whitby and burns it all—toxins, plastics, electronics, rubber, bills, dog collars, love letters— with gleeful disregard of the bylaw enforcers constantly summoned to her intoxicating suburban lot by neighbours engulfed in the stench. Oh, Enji, she might say, take my troubles. Leave nothing here on earth. Nothing inspires joy like your tongue.

"Bhikkhus," says Shakyamuni Buddha, beginning a sermon about change, suffering, and its release. "All is burning. And what is the all that is burning?" He is sitting still near the placid waters of a pond blossoming with pink lotus flowers, closing now slightly, with extraordinary delicacy, with the drawing down of the sun. And we are far from finding a part that endures, but perhaps we are better equipped now to answer this question. What is the all that is burning if everything is burning: Greece, California, Russia, Canada? The last drum of oil pulled from the sands of Alberta, the last combustion engine shot across the sky. Should we simply say the whole world is on fire, from the sun to our toddlers to the swiftly disappearing stars? Yes. But what is the whole world? Surely the Buddha is not asking his bhikkhus for a rendering, an enumeration, of all the things in the universe, as if we could hold and name each and thus say, "Yes, this, too, is burning." Is water burning? Yes. Is space burning? Of course. Is your cool hammock between two jasmine-scented trees burning? Yes. Is your belief in the novel burning? Duh. Was the bodhi tree on fire? Exquisitely. Staring into a candle flame floating in a teacup, a young spectator can barely follow all these riddles; he feels heartsick over a girl he planned to marry but who became sick and died and turned green, to liquid, in the heat. And this young man feels so lonesome and alone—like, "a lone, all one," but stupidly, not intimately, as he feels he should—that the very thought of thinking, of puzzling out an answer to the Buddha's question itself proves tyrannical, like some self-styled King of Totality. And all at once the notion that fire might be divine, natural, earthly, prosaic, godly, knowable, painful, libidinous, resplendent, forbidden, rank, or fate—options, choices, deliberations—squeezes from him a little "yip" heard by those sangha-members seated around him on the blowing weeds and clover. A noise not unsimilar to David's "yip" of dismay in the tent near the Tim Hortons as he dreams, one boiling afternoon during one of humanity's last summers, of his childhood home cracking and collapsing inward, and of other suburban, Tudor-style homes with closed windows and doors, each full of sleeping husbands and wives, snoring cats, booted infants, and thousands of wonderful toys designed to make us giggle and cum—homes dripping with kerosene, drenched in jet fuel, while David dreams of running through the streets, frantic, trying to wake the sleeping lovers and playing babies, show them that all it will take is the spark of a Bic lighter and the whole thing will go up. You can hear him in the distance, on the other side of the hillside, trapped in his own little realm, even here among the sangha, his warnings echoing from the Tim Hortons. And stalking through the assembled masses is none other than T. S. Eliot, Old Possum, Thomas Stearns, looking weary, looking as ancient and dried as Tiresias, as though he has been on a great voyage far from home, and has found his way through a field swept by embers, through tornados of heat, through flames that roared from white to yellow, orange to red to deepest black—clusters of black holes, roiling solar, microwave hot and condominium big. For how long, he doesn't know. It seems he passed David on a suburban street, ranting to the sleeping residents. It seems he staggered through a place of sorrows where Jesus hangs on a cross, and Origen of Alexandria ascends a narrow platform, and Girolamo Savonarola burns on a stake, and dogs melt into the nothing of memes, and cities disappear under nuclear ashes, and Canadians wait in lines in drive-thrus listening to audiobook recordings of *The Life-Changing Magic of Tidying Up* as the planet dies, over and over, no end and no beginning. The small, heart-stricken boy on the hill, missing the one girl in his life he'd pinned his hopes on, barely looks up as Eliot climbs the mound and collapses in front of the Buddha. "I am so tired," he says, in more of a weepy voice than he'd intended. "I am so tired and life is so long. Where is my home? Where is my mother's womb? Where is my sucking thumb? Joy is never with me. There is no one to pluck me from this grief, this burning, this homelessness. What must I burn or solder? What must I cut or excise? What should stay, and what should go into the flame?" And much to Eliot's horror, the Buddha says nothing. "I was a poet," he continues, "because of the great pain of the world, or the great pain of my mind. I was embroiled, engulfed, in a life of language. The stakes were high. It mattered what I thought and said and it mattered what I wrote. I was a poet, and in public, and it mattered, damn it! They put medals around my neck. I tried to offer this up as a witness and tribute and it was all I could do, and it burned me to care as much as I did. Even now the feuds and outrages, the coming and the going, inspires in me a dread of going back. I'm burning. I'm on fire." And the Buddha, with monstrous, unspeakable compassion, again says nothing. Instead, he plunges his hand into the pond beside him and pulls up a pink lotus flower. He holds it silently before him, roots dripping with mud.

# NOTES

MOST OF THE preceding pieces have textual origins that served as sources of inspiration and prompts for lift-off. Readers may be interested in or surprised by these or may want to explore the relationship between the inspiring work and the stuff in this book. Just note that the listed sources below aren't rigid models or codes to decipher hidden meanings (the essential meanings were already in front of you). Writing in the "spirit" of a pre-existing work, literary or otherwise, is a strange transaction; it's an emotional, psychic, and largely indescribable dance between authors. Once done, it is indelible. If you write inside someone else's lines, they live inside you for good.

"Ame ni mo Makezu" shares the name of a very famous, posthumous, and most lovely poem by Kenji Miyazawa (1896–1933), usually translated from the katakana syllabary as "Be Not Defeated by the Rain," "Unperturbed by the Rain," or "Standing Up to the Rain." My piece is a tribute and reimagining of the spirit of the original verse. Despite its ludicrous imagery, it is offered with deep respect for the author and the original.

"Sandōkai, Non-Binary" refers to the "Sandōkai," written in the eighth century CE by the Chán master Shítóu Xīqiān (his Japanese name is Sekitō Kisen). The verse is otherwise known as the "Identity of Relative or Absolute" (or as "Merging of Difference and Unity" or "Harmony of Difference and Unity"). This poem is still studied and chanted by Zen practitioners across the world, close to thirteen hundred years after its writing. The "Sandōkai" points out a seemingly paradoxical nature of reality that the relative, expressed as *ji*, and the absolute, expressed as *ri*, are mutually dependent. It also served, historically, to overcome divisions between the northern and southern schools of Chán. Some excellent commentaries on the "Sandōkai" can be found in Shōhaku Okamura's (b. 1948) *Living by Vow*, Shunryū Suzuki's (1904–1971) *Branching Streams Flow in the Darkness*, and in Bernie Glassman's (1939–2018) *Infinite Circle*.

"Hands and Eyes" is a personal, poetic gloss on Case 89 ("Ungan's 'Hands and Eyes'" or "The Hands and Eyes of the Bodhisattva of Great Compassion") from the *Hekiganroku* (the romaji form of what we call *The Blue Cliff Record* in English). *The Blue Cliff Record* is a series of koans assembled by Yuánwù Kèqín (1063–1135 CE), a member of the Linji school of Chán Buddhism (later developed into the Rinzai sect in Japan). Yuánwù Kèqín is known as Engo Kokugon in Japan. The case begins with Ungan asking Dogo, "Why does the Bodhisattva of Great Mercy [i.e., Avalokiteshvara, Kannon, Kanzeon, Guanyin, etc.] use so many hands and eyes?" and ends with the clearest answer possible: "The entire body is hands and eyes."

"Cadets-in-Training Presentation, Toronto Police College, 2020" refers to some lines in Shì Dàoyuán's *Jǐngdé Chuándēng lù*, also known as *Records of the Transmission of the Lamp*. I was inspired by sections in volume 1: *The Buddhas and Indian Patriarchs*, translated by Randolph S. Whitfield (2015).

"Motivation" quotes from Jack Kerouac's *The Scripture of the Golden Eternity* (1960) and from James Joyce's short story "The Dead."

"The Garbage and Oil Thread," much in the same spirit as "Sandōkai, Non-Binary," offers a reverential reimagining of "Sansui kyō" (or "Sansuigyo"), typically translated as "The Mountains and Rivers Sutra" (or as "The Sutra of Mountains and Water" or "On the Spiritual Discourses of the Mountains and the Water"), one of the ninety-five fascicles of the Shōbōgenzō of Eihei Dōgen zenji (1200–1253 CE), and written in the autumn of 1240 CE. Eihei Dogen was a priest, philosopher, and poet, and brought the Cáodòng zōng (Cáodòng school) of Chán Buddhism (one of the Five Houses of Chán) to Japan in 1227 CE. He is considered the founder of Sōtō Zen, today the largest sect of Zen in Japan and across the globe. In preparing this piece, I consulted and compared translations by Gudo Wafu Nishijima and Chodo Cross, Kazuaki Tanahashi, Rev. Hubert Nearman, Carl Bielefeldt, Andrew Hobai Pekarik, and Brad Warner. I am especially indebted to Shōhaku Okumura's comprehensive *The Mountains and Waters Sutra: A Practitioner's Guide to Dōgen's "Sansuikyo"* (with contributions from Carl Bielefeldt, Gary Snyder, and Isshō Fujita).

"The Hell of Laughter" refers to a phrase within the "Talaputa Sutta: To Talaputa the Actor," found within the Samyutta Nikaya. As per Thanissaro Bhikku's translation, Talaputa is the head of an acting troupe and has a burning question for the Buddha, rendered as thus: "Lord, I have heard that it has been passed down by the ancient teaching lineage of actors that, 'When an actor on the stage, in the midst of a festival, makes people laugh and gives them delight with his imitation of reality, then with the breakup of the body, after death, he is reborn in the company of the laughing devas.' What does the Blessed One have to say about that?" What do you think the Blessed One has to say in response? The piece also references the posthumous collection *Le Spleen de Paris* (*Paris Spleen*), published in 1869, by Charles Baudelaire (1821–1867), who shares with me and Kristen Stewart an April 9 birthday. I dedicate this piece to all my writer friends.

The title "The Horrible Inclemency of Life" was derived from a quotation from Aldous Huxley's novel *Antic Hay* (1923): "Perhaps it's good for one to suffer. Can an artist do anything if he's happy? Would he ever want to do anything? What is art, after all, but a protest against the horrible inclemency of life?"

"Memorial Prayer" draws from "Inspiration Prayer Calling on the Buddhas and Bodhisattvas for Rescue" in *The Tibetan Book of the Dead* (the translation I've used is by Francesca Fremantle and Chögyam Trungpa, released in 2000), as well as contemporary Zen memorial chants. It also references the Assu Sutta (from the Anamatagga-samyutta, or "the unimaginable beginnings of samsara," within the Nidana Vagga of the Samyutta Nikaya, the third division of the Sutta Pitaka). Paolo and Francesca are, of course, Francesca da Rimini and Paolo Malatesta, detailed in Canto V of Dante's *Inferno* as residing in the Second Circle of Hell.

"The Gateless Gate" refers to Wúmén Huìkāi's (1183–1260 CE) *Wúménguān*, frequently translated as *The Gateless Barrier* or, more alliteratively, as *The Gateless Gate*: a compilation of Chán/Zen koans published around 1228 CE. In Japanese, Wúmén Huìkāi is known as Mumon Ekai and his compilation of koans is called *Mumonkan*. The piece included in this book takes its starting point from Mumon's haunting preface to *The Gateless Gate*, as translated by the great teacher Katsuki Sekida (1893–1987) in his *Two Zen Classics: The Gateless Gate and the Blue Cliff Records*.

"Turn Your Anger into Sadness" refers to *kaukritya*, a Sanskrit term indicating regret after wrongdoing: an unwholesome or limiting or hindering mental state to both Theravādin and Mahāyāna Buddhists. The piece also references Niobe, of Greek mythology, whose children were murdered by Artemis and Apollo as punishment for her hubris. After retreating to her place of birth, Mount Sipylus, Niobe was turned to stone, and in this frozen form will weep for her lost children until the mountain crumbles to dust. The Weeping Rock is located in Manisa, in the Republic of Türkiye, and because it pours forth a staining fluid, and because it resembles a woman's face, it is associated with Niobe's sad end.

"In the 2000s" riffs on, and updates, Leonard Michaels's (1933–2003) short story "In the Fifties," from the collection *I Would Have Saved Them If I Could* (1975), while paying homage to the spirit of the memoirs *Ongoingness: The End of a Diary* (2016) by Sarah Manguso and *I Remember* (1970), *I Remember More* (1972), and *More I Remember More* (1973) by Joe Brainard (1942–1994). If there were no copyright concerns, I would preface the work with a line from the bridge to Taylor Swift's song "august" from the album *Folklore* (2020). "In the 2000s" also quotes from Allen Ginsberg's poem "Kaddish" from *Kaddish and Other Poems* (1961).

"There Is Nothing to Dislike" takes its title from Línjì Yìxuán's (d. 866 CE) "There Is Nothing I Dislike," drawn from the *Linji lu* (or *The Record of Linji*). A massively influential figure in Chán/Zen, Línjì Yìxuán is today perhaps better known by his Japanese name, Rinzai Gigen. He was the founder of the Linji school of Chán Buddhism in China and the Rinzai school of Zen in Japan, and influenced the Jogye Order in Korea. "Enlightenment abides nowhere," Línjì is quoted as saying, in a translation by J. C. Cleary. "Therefore, there is no attaining it. What else is there for really great people to be in doubt about? Who is the one before your very eyes functioning? Take hold and act: don't affix names. This is the mystic message. If you can see things this way, there is nothing to despise or avoid."

"The Fire Sermon" is the popular name for the Ādittapariyāya Sutta (within the Salayatana Vagga—"The Section on the Six Sense Bases" of the Samyutta Nikaya, the third division of the Sutta Pitaka). In this sermon, Shakyamuni Buddha describes how grasping, attaching to, taking as real, etc., the senses, their objects, and corresponding mental formations causes suffering, and outlines a process of disenchantment, dispassion, and release. Later glosses on the text claim the subject, fire, was chosen specifically to address those who practised Agnihotri rites—a yajna (ritual) done before a sacred fire, one still practised today. In *The Waste Land* (1922) by T. S. Eliot (1888–1965), "The Fire Sermon" is the name of the third section of the poem. In a footnote, Eliot makes the strange claim that the Ādittapariyāya Sutta is akin to the Sermon on the Mount. This poem also refers to the Parable of the Burning House, detailed in the vital Mahāyāna text *The Lotus Sutra*, mong other sources, and quotes directly from T. S. Eliot's "The Love Song of J. Alfred Prufrock."

All other sources in the text—Origen of Alexandria, Eusebius, King Nebuchadnezzar II, Girolamo Savonarola, Marie Kondo, KC Green, Illyria, etc.—are fairly self-explanatory.

# ACKNOWLEDGEMENTS

ALL ROYALTIES ACCRUED from this book, from its inception to disappearance, will be donated on an annual basis to Fred Victor, a social service charitable organization that fosters long-lasting and positive change in the lives of homeless and low-income people living across Toronto. Thank you for purchasing this book and contributing, in a small way, to people in need. Learn more at fredvictor.org.

Thank you to the Ontario Arts Council and Canada Council for the Arts for generous funding during the creation of this manuscript. Special thanks to Coach House Books (Alana), House of Anansi Press (Kevin and Joshua), and Wolsak & Wynn (Paul) for their assistance through the Recommender Grants for Writers program.

Endless thanks to my editor, Kevin Connolly, my copyeditor, Gil Adamson, and to everyone at House of Anansi Press, especially Leigh Nash, who helped bring this book to life. Thank you to Shivaun Hearne, Ingrid Wu, Jenny McWha, Emma Rhodes, and Rachel Spence.

Thank you to Bardia and Andrew for advice on pitching this

manuscript; to Nate for numerous pushes and title changes; and to members of the short-lived Writing Thing and its post-COVID digital baby: to Benvie, Stephen, Bruce, Anne, Lis, Shawn, Iván, Jose, Nicolas, Allison, etc. Thanks as well to members of Khali for keeping me distracted by fantastical worlds for over six years.

Deep gassho to Ven. Anzan Hoshin roshi and to my instructors in the Practice Council from the White Wind Zen Community at Honzan Dainen-ji in Ottawa, Ontario (Ven. Jinmyo Renge sensei, Ven. Mishin Roelofs godo, Ven. Saigyo Cross ino)—even though this book is a work of poetry and fiction and has absolutely nothing to do with the truth of their teachings, nor the Buddhadharma.

Finally, thank you to my many colleagues throughout my several career moves and mistakes (from Scout to ONCAT to HEQCO to Blueprint), to my hideous friends, and to my family, both in Canada and Scotland—especially Steph, Ken, Susan, Emma, and Bob—for their enduring patience and encouraging support for this indulgent little writing hobby of mine.

An earlier version of "Ame ni mo Makezu" was published in *Train : a poetry journal*, October 2019; an earlier version of "Reasons for My Success" was published in *newpoetry.ca*, May 2018; an earlier version of "The Horrible Inclemency of Life" (originally titled "An Ordinary Childhood") was published in *Ottawater* #14, January 2018; an earlier version of "This Thing I Believe" was published in *Columbia Journal*, #57, May 2018; and an earlier version of "Okay" was published in *talking about strawberries all the time*, April 2019.

Photo credit: Danita Hosking

SPENCER GORDON is the author of the poetry collection *Cruise Missile Liberals* (Nightwood Editions, 2017) and the short story collection *Cosmo* (Coach House Books, 2012). He co-founded and edited the literary journal *The Puritan* for a decade and has taught writing at Humber College, OCAD University, George Brown College and the University of Toronto. He works as a Principal Associate for Blueprint, a non-profit research organization dedicated to solving public policy challenges. Follow him on Twitter/X at @spencergordon and visit his rudimentary website at spencer-gordon.com.